The Man Who Knew Too Much

Gilbert Keith Chesterton

I. THE FACE IN THE TARGET

Harold March, the rising reviewer and social critic, was walking vigorously across a great tableland of moors and commons, the horizon of which was fringed with the far-off woods of the famous estate of Torwood Park. He was a good-looking young man in tweeds, with very pale curly hair and pale clear eyes. Walking in wind and sun in the very landscape of liberty, he was still young enough to remember his politics and not merely try to forget them. For his errand at Torwood Park was a political one; it was the place of appointment named by no less a person than the Chancellor of the Exchequer, Sir Howard Horne, then introducing his so-called Socialist budget, and prepared to expound it in an interview with so promising a penman. Harold March was the sort of man who knows everything about politics, and nothing about politicians. He also knew a great deal about art, letters, philosophy, and general culture; about almost everything, indeed, except the world he was living in.

Abruptly, in the middle of those sunny and windy flats, he came upon a sort of cleft almost narrow enough to be called a crack in the land. It was just large enough to be the water-course for a small stream which vanished at intervals under green tunnels of undergrowth, as if in a dwarfish forest. Indeed, he had an odd feeling as if he were a giant looking over the valley of the pygmies. When he dropped into the hollow, however, the impression was lost; the rocky banks, though hardly above the height of a cottage, hung over and had the profile of a precipice. As he began to wander down the course of the stream, in idle but romantic curiosity, and saw the water shining in short strips between the great gray boulders and bushes as soft as great green mosses, he fell into quite an opposite vein of fantasy. It was rather as if the earth had opened and swallowed him into a sort of underworld of dreams. And when he became conscious of a human figure dark against the silver stream, sitting on a large boulder and looking rather like a large bird, it was perhaps with some of the premonitions proper to a man who meets the strangest friendship of his life.

The man was apparently fishing; or at least was fixed in a fisherman's attitude with more than a fisherman's immobility. March was able to examine the man almost as if he had been a statue for some minutes before the statue spoke. He was a tall, fair man, cadaverous, and a little lackadaisical, with heavy eyelids and a highbridged nose. When his face was shaded with his wide white hat, his light mustache and lithe figure gave him a look of youth. But the Panama lay on the moss beside him; and the spectator could see that his brow was prematurely bald; and this, combined with a certain hollowness about the eyes, had an air of headwork and even headache. But the most curious thing about him, realized after a short scrutiny, was that, though he looked like a fisherman, he was not fishing.

He was holding, instead of a rod, something that might have been a landing-net which some fishermen use, but which was much more like the ordinary toy net which children carry, and which they generally use indifferently for shrimps or butterflies. He was dipping this into the water at intervals, gravely regarding its harvest of weed or mud, and emptying it out again.

"No, I haven't caught anything," he remarked, calmly, as if answering an unspoken query. "When I do I have to throw it back again; especially the big fish. But some of the little beasts interest me when I get 'em."

"A scientific interest, I suppose?" observed March.

"Of a rather amateurish sort, I fear," answered the strange fisherman. "I have a sort of hobby about what they call 'phenomena of phosphorescence.' But it would be rather awkward to go about in society carrying stinking fish."

"I suppose it would," said March, with a smile.

"Rather odd to enter a drawing-room carrying a large luminous cod," continued the stranger, in his listless way. "How quaint it would be if one could carry it about like a lantern, or have little sprats for candles. Some of the seabeasts would really be very pretty like lampshades; the blue sea-snail that glitters all over like starlight; and some of the red starfish really shine like red stars. But, naturally, I'm not looking for them here."

March thought of asking him what he was looking for; but, feeling unequal to a technical discussion at least as deep as the deep-sea fishes, he returned to more ordinary topics.

"Delightful sort of hole this is," he said. "This little dell and river here. It's like those places Stevenson talks about, where something ought to happen."

"I know," answered the other. "I think it's because the place itself, so to speak, seems to happen and not merely to exist. Perhaps that's what old Picasso and some of the Cubists are trying to express by angles and jagged lines. Look at that wall like low cliffs that juts forward just at right angles to the slope of turf sweeping up to it. That's like a silent collision. It's like a breaker and the back-wash of a wave."

March looked at the low-browed crag overhanging the green slope and nodded. He was interested in a man who turned so easily from the technicalities of science to those of art; and asked him if he admired the new angular artists.

"As I feel it, the Cubists are not Cubist enough," replied the stranger. "I mean they're not thick enough. By making things mathematical they make them thin. Take the living lines out of that landscape, simplify it to a right angle, and you flatten it out to a mere diagram on paper. Diagrams have their own beauty; but it is of just the other sort. They stand for the unalterable things; the calm, eternal, mathematical sort of truths; what somebody calls the 'white radiance of'—"

He stopped, and before the next word came something had happened almost too quickly and completely to be realized. From behind the overhanging rock came a noise and rush like that of a railway train; and a great motor car appeared. It topped the crest of cliff, black against the sun, like a battle-chariot rushing to destruction in some wild epic. March automatically put out his hand in one futile gesture, as if to catch a falling tea-cup in a drawing-room.

For the fraction of a flash it seemed to leave the ledge of rock like a flying ship; then the very sky seemed to turn over like a wheel, and it lay a ruin amid the tall grasses below, a line of gray smoke going up slowly from it into the silent air. A little lower the figure of a man with gray hair lay tumbled down the steep green slope, his limbs lying all at random, and his face turned away.

The eccentric fisherman dropped his net and walked swiftly toward the spot, his new acquaintance following him. As they drew near there seemed a sort of monstrous irony in the fact that the dead machine was still throbbing and thundering as busily as a factory, while the man lay so still.

He was unquestionably dead. The blood flowed in the grass from a hopelessly fatal fracture at the back of the skull; but the face, which was turned to the sun, was uninjured and strangely arresting in itself. It was one of those cases of a strange face so unmistakable as to feel familiar. We feel, somehow, that we ought to recognize it, even though we do not. It was of the broad, square sort with great jaws, almost like that of a highly intellectual ape; the wide mouth shut so tight as to be traced by a mere line; the nose short with the sort of nostrils that seem to gape with an appetite for the air. The oddest thing about the face was that one of the eyebrows was cocked up at a much sharper angle than the other. March thought he had never seen a face so naturally alive as that dead one. And its ugly energy seemed all the stranger for its halo of hoary hair. Some papers lay half fallen out of the pocket, and from among them March extracted a card-case. He read the name on the card aloud.

"Sir Humphrey Turnbull. I'm sure I've heard that name somewhere."

His companion only gave a sort of a little sigh and was silent for a moment, as if ruminating, then he merely said, "The poor fellow is quite gone," and added some scientific terms in which his auditor once more found himself out of his depth.

"As things are," continued the same curiously well-informed person, "it will be more legal for us to leave the body as it is until the police are informed. In fact, I think it will be well if nobody except the police is informed. Don't be surprised if I seem to be keeping it dark from some of our neighbors round here." Then, as if prompted to regularize his rather abrupt confidence, he said: "I've come down to see my cousin at Torwood; my name is Horne Fisher. Might be a pun on my pottering about here, mightn't it?"

"Is Sir Howard Horne your cousin?" asked March. "I'm going to Torwood Park to see him myself; only about his public work, of course, and the wonderful stand he is making for his principles. I think this Budget is the greatest thing in English history. If it fails, it will be the most heroic failure in English history. Are you an admirer of your great kinsman, Mr. Fisher?"

"Rather," said Mr. Fisher. "He's the best shot I know."

Then, as if sincerely repentant of his nonchalance, he added, with a sort of enthusiasm:

"No, but really, he's a beautiful shot."

As if fired by his own words, he took a sort of leap at the ledges of the rock above him, and scaled them with a sudden agility in startling contrast to his general lassitude. He had stood for some seconds on the headland above, with his aquiline profile under the Panama hat relieved against the sky and peering over the countryside before his companion had collected himself sufficiently to scramble up after him.

The level above was a stretch of common turf on which the tracks of the fated car were plowed plainly enough; but the brink of it was broken as with rocky teeth; broken boulders of all shapes and sizes lay near the edge; it was almost incredible that any one could have deliberately driven into such a death trap, especially in broad daylight.

"I can't make head or tail of it," said March. "Was he blind? Or blind drunk?"

"Neither, by the look of him," replied the other.

"Then it was suicide."

"It doesn't seem a cozy way of doing it," remarked the man called Fisher. "Besides, I don't fancy poor old Puggy would commit suicide, somehow."

"Poor old who?" inquired the wondering journalist. "Did you know this unfortunate man?"

"Nobody knew him exactly," replied Fisher, with some vagueness. "But one knew him, of course. He'd been a terror in his time, in Parliament and the courts, and so on; especially in that row about the aliens who were deported as undesirables, when he wanted one of 'em hanged for murder. He was so sick about it that he retired from the bench. Since then he mostly motored about by himself; but he was coming to Torwood, too, for the week-end; and I don't see why he should deliberately break his neck almost at the very door. I believe Hoggs—I mean my cousin Howard—was coming down specially to meet him."

"Torwood Park doesn't belong to your cousin?" inquired March.

"No; it used to belong to the Winthrops, you know," replied the other. "Now a new man's got it; a man from Montreal named Jenkins. Hoggs comes for the shooting; I told you he was a lovely shot."

This repeated eulogy on the great social statesman affected Harold March as if somebody had defined Napoleon as a distinguished player of nap. But he had another half-formed impression struggling in this flood of unfamiliar things, and he brought it to the surface before it could vanish.

"Jenkins," he repeated. "Surely you don't mean Jefferson Jenkins, the social reformer? I mean the man who's fighting for the new cottage-estate scheme. It would be as interesting to meet him as any Cabinet Minister in the world, if you'll excuse my saying so."

"Yes; Hoggs told him it would have to be cottages," said Fisher. "He said the breed of cattle had improved too often, and people were beginning to laugh. And, of course, you must hang a peerage on to something; though the poor chap hasn't got it yet. Hullo, here's somebody else."

They had started walking in the tracks of the car, leaving it behind them in the hollow, still humming horribly like a huge insect that had killed a man. The tracks took them to the corner of the road, one arm of which went on in the same line toward the distant gates of the park. It was clear that the car had been driven down the long straight road, and then, instead of turning with the road to the left, had gone straight on over the turf to its doom. But it was not this discovery that had riveted Fisher's eye, but something even more solid. At the angle of the white road a dark and solitary figure was standing almost as still as a finger post. It was that of a big man in rough shooting-clothes, bareheaded, and with tousled curly hair that gave him a rather wild look. On a nearer approach this first more fantastic impression faded; in a full light the figure took on more conventional colors, as of an ordinary gentleman who happened to have come out without a hat and without very studiously brushing his hair. But the massive stature remained, and something deep and even cavernous about the setting of the eyes redeemed his animal good looks from the commonplace. But March had no time to study the man more closely, for, much to his astonishment, his guide merely observed, "Hullo, Jack!" and walked past him as if he had indeed been a signpost, and without attempting to inform him of the catastrophe beyond the rocks. It was relatively a small thing, but it was only the first in a string of singular antics on which his new and eccentric friend was leading him.

The man they had passed looked after them in rather a suspicious fashion, but Fisher continued serenely on his way along the straight road that ran past the gates of the great estate.

"That's John Burke, the traveler," he condescended to explain. "I expect you've heard of him; shoots big game and all that. Sorry I couldn't stop to introduce you, but I dare say you'll meet him later on."

"I know his book, of course," said March, with renewed interest. "That is certainly a fine piece of description, about their being only conscious of the closeness of the elephant when the colossal head blocked out the moon."

"Yes, young Halkett writes jolly well, I think. What? Didn't you know Halkett wrote Burke's book for him? Burke can't use anything except a gun; and you can't write with that. Oh, he's genuine enough in his way, you know, as brave as a lion, or a good deal braver by all accounts."

"You seem to know all about him," observed March, with a rather bewildered laugh, "and about a good many other people."

Fisher's bald brow became abruptly corrugated, and a curious expression came into his eyes.

"I know too much," he said. "That's what's the matter with me. That's what's the matter with all of us, and the whole show; we know too much. Too much about one another; too much about ourselves. That's why I'm really interested, just now, about one thing that I don't know."

"And that is?" inquired the other.

"Why that poor fellow is dead."

They had walked along the straight road for nearly a mile, conversing at intervals in this fashion; and March had a singular sense of the whole world being turned inside out. Mr. Horne Fisher did not especially abuse his friends and relatives in fashionable society; of some of them he spoke with affection. But they seemed to be an entirely new set of men and women, who happened to have the same nerves as the men and women mentioned most often in the newspapers. Yet no fury of revolt could have seemed to him more utterly revolutionary than this cold familiarity. It was like daylight on the other side of stage scenery.

They reached the great lodge gates of the park, and, to March's surprise, passed them and continued along the interminable white, straight road. But he was himself too early for his appointment with Sir Howard, and was not disinclined to see the end of his new friend's experiment, whatever it might be. They had long left the moorland behind them, and half the white road was gray in the great shadow of the Torwood pine forests, themselves like gray bars shuttered against the sunshine and within, amid that clear noon, manufacturing their own midnight. Soon, however, rifts began to appear in them like gleams of colored windows; the trees thinned and fell away as the road went forward, showing the wild, irregular copses in which, as Fisher said, the house-party had been blazing away all day. And about two hundred yards farther on they came to the first turn of the road.

At the corner stood a sort of decayed inn with the dingy sign of The Grapes. The signboard was dark and indecipherable by now, and hung black against the sky and the gray moorland beyond, about as inviting as a gallows. March remarked that it looked like a tavern for vinegar instead of wine.

"A good phrase," said Fisher, "and so it would be if you were silly enough to drink wine in it. But the beer is very good, and so is the brandy."

March followed him to the bar parlor with some wonder, and his dim sense of repugnance was not dismissed by the first sight of the innkeeper, who was widely different from the genial innkeepers of romance, a bony man, very silent behind a black mustache, but with black, restless eyes. Taciturn as he was, the investigator succeeded at last in extracting a scrap of information from him, by dint of ordering beer and talking to him persistently and minutely on the subject of motor cars. He evidently regarded the innkeeper as in some singular way an authority on motor cars; as being deep in the secrets of the mechanism, management, and mismanagement of motor cars; holding the man all the time with a glittering eye like the Ancient Mariner. Out of all this rather mysterious conversation there did emerge at last a sort of admission that one particular motor car, of a given description, had stopped before the inn about an hour before, and that an elderly man had alighted, requiring some mechanical assistance. Asked if the visitor required any other assistance, the innkeeper said shortly that the old gentleman had filled his flask and taken a packet of sandwiches. And with these words the somewhat inhospitable host had walked hastily out of the bar, and they heard him banging doors in the dark interior.

Fisher's weary eye wandered round the dusty and dreary inn parlor and rested dreamily on a glass case containing a stuffed bird, with a gun hung on hooks above it, which seemed to be its only ornament.

"Puggy was a humorist," he observed, "at least in his own rather grim style. But it seems rather too grim a joke for a man to buy a packet of sandwiches when he is just going to commit suicide."

"If you come to that," answered March, "it isn't very usual for a man to buy a packet of sandwiches when he's just outside the door of a grand house he's going to stop at."

"No . . . no," repeated Fisher, almost mechanically; and then suddenly cocked his eye at his interlocutor with a much livelier expression.

"By Jove! that's an idea. You're perfectly right. And that suggests a very queer idea, doesn't it?"

There was a silence, and then March started with irrational nervousness as the door of the inn was flung open and another man walked rapidly to the counter. He had struck it with a coin and called out for brandy before he saw the other two guests, who were sitting at a bare wooden table under the window. When he turned about with a rather wild stare, March had yet another unexpected emotion, for his guide hailed the man as Hoggs and introduced him as Sir Howard Horne.

He looked rather older than his boyish portraits in the illustrated papers, as is the way of politicians; his flat, fair hair was touched with gray, but his face was almost comically round, with a Roman nose which, when combined with his quick, bright eyes, raised a vague reminiscence of a parrot. He had a cap rather at the back of his head and a gun under his arm. Harold March had imagined many things about his meeting with the great political reformer, but he had never pictured him with a gun under his arm, drinking brandy in a public house.

"So you're stopping at Jink's, too," said Fisher. "Everybody seems to be at Jink's."

"Yes," replied the Chancellor of the Exchequer. "Jolly good shooting. At least all of it that isn't Jink's shooting. I never knew a chap with such good shooting that was such a bad shot. Mind you, he's a jolly good fellow and all that; I don't say a word against him. But he never learned to hold a gun when he was packing pork or whatever he did. They say he shot the cockade off his own servant's hat; just like him to have cockades, of course. He shot the weathercock off his own ridiculous gilded summerhouse. It's the only cock he'll ever kill, I should think. Are you coming up there now?"

Fisher said, rather vaguely, that he was following soon, when he had fixed something up; and the Chancellor of the Exchequer left the inn. March fancied he had been a little upset or impatient when he called for the brandy; but he had talked himself back into a satisfactory state, if the talk had not been quite what his literary visitor had expected. Fisher, a few minutes afterward, slowly led the way out of the tavern and stood in the middle of the road, looking down in the direction from which they had traveled. Then he walked back about two hundred yards in that direction and stood still again.

"I should think this is about the place," he said.

"What place?" asked his companion.

"The place where the poor fellow was killed," said Fisher, sadly.

"What do you mean?" demanded March.

"He was smashed up on the rocks a mile and a half from here."

"No, he wasn't," replied Fisher. "He didn't fall on the rocks at all. Didn't you notice that he only fell on the slope of soft grass underneath? But I saw that he had a bullet in him already."

Then after a pause he added:

"He was alive at the inn, but he was dead long before he came to the rocks. So he was shot as he drove his car down this strip of straight road, and I should think somewhere about here. After that, of course, the car went straight on with nobody to stop or turn it. It's really a very cunning dodge in its way; for the body would be found far away, and most people would say, as you do, that it was an accident to a motorist. The murderer must have been a clever brute."

"But wouldn't the shot be heard at the inn or somewhere?" asked

March.

"It would be heard. But it would not be noticed. That," continued the investigator, "is where he was clever again. Shooting was going on all over the place all day; very likely he timed his shot so as to drown it in a number of others. Certainly he was a first-class criminal. And he was something else as well."

"What do you mean?" asked his companion, with a creepy premonition of something coming, he knew not why.

"He was a first-class shot," said Fisher. He had turned his back abruptly and was walking down a narrow, grassy lane, little more than a cart track, which lay opposite the inn and marked the end of the great estate and the beginning of the open moors. March plodded after him with the same idle perseverance, and found him staring through a gap in giant weeds and thorns at the flat face of a painted paling. From behind the paling rose the great gray columns of a row of poplars, which filled the heavens above them with dark-green shadow and shook faintly in a wind which had sunk slowly into a breeze. The afternoon was already deepening into evening, and the titanic shadows of the poplars lengthened over a third of the landscape.

"Are you a first-class criminal?" asked Fisher, in a friendly tone. "I'm afraid I'm not. But I think I can manage to be a sort of fourth-rate burglar."

And before his companion could reply he had managed to swing himself up and over the fence; March followed without much bodily effort, but with considerable mental disturbance. The poplars grew so close against the fence that they had some difficulty in slipping past them, and beyond the poplars they could see only a high hedge of laurel, green and lustrous in the level sun. Something in this limitation by a series of living walls made him feel as if he were really entering a shattered house instead of an open field. It was as if he came in by a disused door or window and found the way blocked by furniture. When they had circumvented the laurel hedge, they came out on a sort of terrace of turf, which fell by one green step to an oblong lawn like a bowling green. Beyond this was the only building in sight, a low conservatory, which seemed far away from anywhere, like a glass cottage standing in its own fields in fairyland. Fisher knew that lonely look of the outlying parts of a great house well enough. He realized that it is more of a satire on aristocracy than if it were choked with weeds and littered with ruins. For it is not neglected and yet it is deserted; at any rate, it is disused. It is regularly swept and garnished for a master who never comes.

Looking over the lawn, however, he saw one object which he had not apparently expected. It was a sort of tripod supporting a large disk like the round top of a table tipped sideways, and it was not until they had dropped on to the lawn and walked across to look at it that March realized that it was a target. It was worn and weatherstained; the gay colors of its concentric rings were faded; possibly it had been set up in those far-off Victorian days when there was a fashion of archery. March had one of his vague visions of ladies in cloudy crinolines and gentlemen in outlandish hats and whiskers revisiting that lost garden like ghosts.

Fisher, who was peering more closely at the target, startled him by an exclamation.

"Hullo!" he said. "Somebody has been peppering this thing with shot, after all, and quite lately, too. Why, I believe old Jink's been trying to improve his bad shooting here."

"Yes, and it looks as if it still wanted improving," answered March, laughing. "Not one of these shots is anywhere near the bull's-eye; they seem just scattered about in the wildest way."

"In the wildest way," repeated Fisher, still peering intently at the target. He seemed merely to assent, but March fancied his eye was shining under its sleepy lid and that he straightened his stooping figure with a strange effort.

"Excuse me a moment," he said, feeling in his pockets. "I think I've got some of my chemicals; and after that we'll go up to the house." And he stooped again over the target, putting something with his finger over each of the shot-holes, so far as March could see merely a dull-gray smear. Then they went through the gathering twilight up the long green avenues to the great house.

Here again, however, the eccentric investigator did not enter by the front door. He walked round the house until he found a window open, and, leaping into it, introduced his friend to what appeared to be the gun-room. Rows of the regular instruments for bringing down birds stood against the walls; but across a table in the window lay one or two weapons of a heavier and more formidable pattern.

"Hullo! these are Burke's big-game rifles," said Fisher. "I never knew he kept them here." He lifted one of them, examined it briefly, and put it down again, frowning heavily. Almost as he did so a strange young man came hurriedly into the room. He was dark and sturdy, with a bumpy forehead and a bulldog jaw, and he spoke with a curt apology.

"I left Major Burke's guns here," he said, "and he wants them packed up. He's going away to-night."

And he carried off the two rifles without casting a glance at the stranger; through the open window they could see his short, dark figure walking away across the glimmering garden. Fisher got out of the window again and stood looking after him.

"That's Halkett, whom I told you about," he said. "I knew he was a sort of secretary and had to do with Burke's papers; but I never knew he had anything to do with his guns. But he's just the sort of silent, sensible little devil who might be very good at anything; the sort of man you know for years before you find he's a chess champion."

He had begun to walk in the direction of the disappearing secretary, and they soon came within sight of the rest of the house-party talking and laughing on the lawn. They could see the tall figure and loose mane of the lion-hunter dominating the little group.

"By the way," observed Fisher, "when we were talking about Burke and Halkett, I said that a man couldn't very well write with a gun. Well, I'm not so sure now. Did you ever hear of an artist so clever that he could draw with a gun? There's a wonderful chap loose about here."

Sir Howard hailed Fisher and his friend the journalist with almost boisterous amiability. The latter was presented to Major Burke and Mr. Halkett and also (by way of a parenthesis) to his host, Mr. Jenkins, a commonplace little man in loud tweeds, whom everybody else seemed to treat with a sort of affection, as if he were a baby.

The irrepressible Chancellor of the Exchequer was still talking about the birds he had brought down, the birds that Burke and Halkett had brought down, and the birds that Jenkins, their host, had failed to bring down. It seemed to be a sort of sociable monomania.

"You and your big game," he ejaculated, aggressively, to Burke. "Why, anybody could shoot big game. You want to be a shot to shoot small game."

"Quite so," interposed Horne Fisher. "Now if only a hippopotamus could fly up in the air out of that bush, or you preserved flying elephants on the estate, why, then—"

"Why even Jink might hit that sort of bird," cried Sir Howard, hilariously slapping his host on the back. "Even he might hit a haystack or a hippopotamus."

"Look here, you fellows," said Fisher. "I want you to come along with me for a minute and shoot at something else. Not a hippopotamus. Another kind of queer animal I've found on the estate. It's an animal with three legs and one eye, and it's all the colors of the rainbow."

"What the deuce are you talking about?" asked Burke.

"You come along and see," replied Fisher, cheerfully.

Such people seldom reject anything nonsensical, for they are always seeking for something new. They gravely rearmed themselves from the gun-room and trooped along at the tail of their guide, Sir Howard only pausing, in a sort of ecstasy, to point out the celebrated gilt summerhouse on which the gilt weathercock still stood crooked. It was dusk turning to dark by the time they reached the remote green by the poplars and accepted the new and aimless game of shooting at the old mark.

The last light seemed to fade from the lawn, and the poplars against the sunset were like great plumes upon a purple hearse, when the futile procession finally curved round, and came out in front of the target. Sir Howard again slapped his host on the shoulder, shoving him playfully forward to take the first shot. The shoulder and arm he touched seemed unnaturally stiff and angular. Mr. Jenkins was holding his gun in an attitude more awkward than any that his satiric friends had seen or expected.

At the same instant a horrible scream seemed to come from nowhere. It was so unnatural and so unsuited to the scene that it might have been made by some inhuman thing flying on wings above them or eavesdropping in the dark woods beyond. But Fisher knew that it had started and stopped on the pale lips of Jefferson Jenkins, of Montreal, and no one at that moment catching sight of Jefferson Jenkins's face would have complained that it was commonplace. The next moment a torrent of guttural but good-humored oaths came from Major Burke as he and the two other men saw what was in front of them. The target stood up in the dim grass like a dark goblin grinning at them, and it was literally grinning. It had two eyes like stars, and in similar livid points of light were picked out the two upturned and open nostrils and the two ends of the wide and tight mouth. A few white dots above each eye indicated the hoary eyebrows; and one of them ran upward almost erect. It was a brilliant caricature done in bright dotted lines and March knew of whom. It shone in the shadowy grass, smeared with sea fire as if one of the submarine monsters had crawled into the twilight garden; but it had the head of a dead man.

"It's only luminous paint," said Burke. "Old Fisher's been having a joke with that phosphorescent stuff of his."

"Seems to be meant for old Puggy"' observed Sir Howard. "Hits him off very well."

With that they all laughed, except Jenkins. When they had all done, he made a noise like the first effort of an animal to laugh, and Horne Fisher suddenly strode across to him and said:

"Mr. Jenkins, I must speak to you at once in private."

It was by the little watercourse in the moors, on the slope under the hanging rock, that March met his new friend Fisher, by appointment, shortly after the ugly and almost grotesque scene that had broken up the group in the garden.

"It was a monkey-trick of mine," observed Fisher, gloomily, "putting phosphorus on the target; but the only chance to make him jump was to give him the horrors suddenly. And when he saw the face he'd shot at shining on the target he practiced on, all lit up with an infernal light, he did jump. Quite enough for my own intellectual satisfaction."

"I'm afraid I don't quite understand even now," said March, "exactly what he did or why he did it."

"You ought to," replied Fisher, with his rather dreary smile, "for you gave me the first suggestion yourself. Oh yes, you did; and it was a very shrewd one. You said a man wouldn't take sandwiches with him to dine at a great house. It was quite true; and the inference was that, though he was going there, he didn't mean to dine there. Or, at any rate, that he might not be dining there. It occurred to me at once that he probably expected the visit to be unpleasant, or the reception doubtful, or something that would prevent his accepting hospitality. Then it struck me that Turnbull was a terror to certain shady characters in the past, and that he had come down to identify and denounce one of them. The chances at the start pointed to the host—that is, Jenkins. I'm morally certain now that Jenkins was the undesirable alien Turnbull wanted to convict in another shooting-affair, but you see the shooting gentleman had another shot in his locker."

"But you said he would have to be a very good shot," protested

March.

"Jenkins is a very good shot," said Fisher. "A very good shot who can pretend to be a very bad shot. Shall I tell you the second hint I hit on, after yours, to make me think it was Jenkins? It was my cousin's account of his bad shooting. He'd shot a cockade off a hat and a weathercock off a building. Now, in fact, a man must shoot very well indeed to shoot so badly as that. He must shoot very neatly to hit the cockade and not the head, or even the hat. If the shots had really gone at random, the chances are a thousand to one that they would not have hit such prominent and picturesque objects. They were chosen because they were prominent and picturesque objects. They make a story to go the round of society. He keeps the crooked weathercock in the summerhouse to perpetuate the story of a legend. And then he lay in wait with his evil eye and wicked gun, safely ambushed behind the legend of his own incompetence.

"But there is more than that. There is the summerhouse itself. I mean there is the whole thing. There's all that Jenkins gets chaffed about, the gilding and the gaudy colors and all the vulgarity that's supposed to stamp him as an upstart. Now, as a matter of fact, upstarts generally don't do this. God knows there's enough of 'em in society; and one knows 'em well enough. And this is the very last thing they do. They're generally only too keen to know the right thing and do it; and they instantly put themselves body and soul into the hands of art decorators and art experts, who do the whole thing for them. There's hardly another millionaire alive who has the moral courage to have a gilt monogram on a chair like that one in the gun-room. For that matter, there's the name as well as the monogram. Names like Tompkins and Jenkins and Jinks are funny without being vulgar; I mean they are vulgar without being common. If you prefer it, they are commonplace without being common. They are just the names to be chosen to look ordinary, but they're really rather extraordinary. Do you know many people called Tompkins? It's a good deal rarer than Talbot. It's pretty much the same with the comic clothes of the parvenu. Jenkins dresses like a character in Punch. But that's because he is a character in Punch. I mean he's a fictitious character. He's a fabulous animal. He doesn't exist.

"Have you ever considered what it must be like to be a man who doesn't exist? I mean to be a man with a fictitious character that he has to keep up at the expense not merely of personal talents: To be a new kind of hypocrite hiding a talent in a new kind of napkin. This man has chosen his hypocrisy very ingeniously; it was really a new one. A subtle villain has dressed up as a dashing gentleman and a worthy business man and a philanthropist and a saint; but the loud checks of a comical little cad were really rather a new disguise. But the disguise must be very irksome to a man who can really do things. This is a dexterous little cosmopolitan guttersnipe who can do scores of things, not only shoot, but draw and paint, and probably play the fiddle. Now a man like that may find the hiding of his talents useful; but he could never help wanting to use them where they were useless. If he can draw, he will draw absent-mindedly on blotting paper. I suspect this rascal has often drawn poor old Puggy's face on blotting paper. Probably he began doing it in blots as he afterward did it in dots, or rather shots. It was the same sort of thing; he found a disused target in a deserted yard and couldn't resist indulging in a little secret shooting, like secret drinking. You thought the shots all scattered and irregular, and so they were; but not accidental. No two distances were alike; but the different points were exactly where he wanted to put them. There's nothing needs such mathematical precision as a wild caricature. I've dabbled a little in drawing myself, and I assure you that to put one dot where you want it is a marvel with a pen close to a piece of paper. It was a miracle to do it across a garden with a gun. But a man who can work those miracles will always itch to work them, if it's only in the dark."

After a pause March observed, thoughtfully, "But he couldn't have brought him down like a bird with one of those little guns."

"No; that was why I went into the gun-room," replied Fisher. "He did it with one of Burke's rifles, and Burke thought he knew the sound of it. That's why he rushed out without a hat, looking so wild. He saw nothing but a car passing quickly, which he followed for a little way, and then concluded he'd made a mistake."

There was another silence, during which Fisher sat on a great stone as motionless as on their first meeting, and watched the gray and silver river eddying past under the bushes. Then March said, abruptly, "Of course he knows the truth now."

"Nobody knows the truth but you and I," answered Fisher, with a certain softening in his voice. "And I don't think you and I will ever quarrel."

"What do you mean?" asked March, in an altered accent. "What have you done about it?"

Horne Fisher continued to gaze steadily at the eddying stream. At last he said, "The police have proved it was a motor accident."

"But you know it was not."

"I told you that I know too much," replied Fisher, with his eye on the river. "I know that, and I know a great many other things. I know the atmosphere and the way the whole thing works. I know this fellow has succeeded in making himself something incurably commonplace and comic. I know you can't get up a persecution of old Toole or Little Tich. If I were to tell Hoggs or Halkett that old Jink was an assassin, they would almost die of laughter before my eyes. Oh, I don't say their laughter's quite innocent, though it's genuine in its way. They want old Jink, and they couldn't do without him. I don't say I'm quite innocent. I like Hoggs; I don't want him to be down and out; and he'd be done for if Jink can't pay for his coronet. They were devilish near the line at the last election. But the only real objection to it is that it's impossible. Nobody would believe it; it's not in the picture. The crooked weathercock would always turn it into a joke."

"Don't you think this is infamous?" asked March, quietly.

"I think a good many things," replied the other. "If you people ever happen to blow the whole tangle of society to hell with dynamite, I don't know that the human race will be much the worse. But don't be too hard on me merely because I know what society is. That's why I moon away my time over things like stinking fish."

There was a pause as he settled himself down again by the stream; and then he added:

"I told you before I had to throw back the big fish."

II. THE VANISHING PRINCE

This tale begins among a tangle of tales round a name that is at once recent and legendary. The name is that of Michael O'Neill, popularly called Prince Michael, partly because he claimed descent from ancient Fenian princes, and partly because he was credited with a plan to make himself prince president of Ireland, as the last Napoleon did of France. He was undoubtedly a gentleman of honorable pedigree and of many accomplishments, but two of his accomplishments emerged from all the rest. He had a talent for appearing when he was not wanted and a talent for disappearing when he was wanted, especially when he was wanted by the police. It may be added that his disappearances were more dangerous than his appearances. In the latter he seldom went beyond the sensational—pasting up seditious placards, tearing down official placards, making flamboyant speeches, or unfurling forbidden flags. But in order to effect the former he would sometimes fight for his freedom with startling energy, from which men were sometimes lucky to escape with a broken head instead of a broken neck. His most famous feats of escape, however, were due to dexterity and not to violence. On a cloudless summer morning he had come down a country road white with dust, and, pausing outside a farmhouse, had told the farmer's daughter, with elegant indifference, that the local police were in pursuit of him. The girl's name was Bridget Royce, a somber and even sullen type of beauty, and she looked at him darkly, as if in doubt, and said, "Do you want me to hide you?" Upon which he only laughed, leaped lightly over the stone wall, and strode toward the farm, merely throwing over his shoulder the remark, "Thank you, I have generally been quite capable of hiding myself." In which proceeding he acted with a tragic ignorance of the nature of women; and there fell on his path in that sunshine a shadow of doom.

While he disappeared through the farmhouse the girl remained for a few moments looking up the road, and two perspiring policemen came plowing up to the door where she stood. Though still angry, she was still silent, and a quarter of an hour later the officers had searched the house and were already inspecting the kitchen garden and cornfield behind it. In the ugly reaction of her mood she might have been tempted even to point out the fugitive, but for a small difficulty that she had no more notion than the policemen had of where he could possibly have gone. The kitchen garden was inclosed by a very low wall, and the cornfield beyond lay aslant like a square patch on a great green hill on which he could still have been seen even as a dot in the distance. Everything stood solid in its familiar place; the apple tree was too small to support or hide a climber; the only shed stood open and obviously empty; there was no sound save the droning of summer flies and the occasional flutter of a bird unfamiliar enough to be surprised by the scarecrow in the field; there was scarcely a shadow save a few blue lines that fell from the thin tree; every detail was picked out by the brilliant day light as if in a microscope. The girl described the scene later, with all the passionate realism of her race, and, whether or no the policemen had a similar eye for the picturesque, they had at least an eye for the facts of the case, and were compelled to give up the chase and retire from the scene. Bridget Royce remained as if in a trance, staring at the sunlit garden in which a man had just vanished like a fairy. She was still in a sinister mood, and the miracle took in her mind a character of unfriendliness and fear, as if the fairy were decidedly a bad fairy. The sun upon the glittering garden depressed her more than the darkness, but she continued to stare at it. Then the world itself went half-witted and she screamed. The scarecrow moved in the sun light. It had stood with its back to her in a battered old black hat and a tattered garment, and with all its tatters flying, it strode away across the hill.

She did not analyze the audacious trick by which the man had turned to his advantage the subtle effects of the expected and the obvious; she was still under the cloud of more individual complexities, and she noticed most of all that the vanishing scarecrow did not even turn to look at the farm. And the fates that were running so adverse to his fantastic career of freedom ruled that his next adventure, though it had the same success in another quarter, should increase the danger in this quarter. Among the many similar adventures related of him in this manner it is also said that some days afterward another girl, named Mary Cregan, found him concealed on the farm where she worked; and if the story is true, she must also have had the shock of an uncanny experience, for when she was busy at some lonely task in the yard she heard a voice speaking out of the well, and found that the eccentric had managed to drop himself into the bucket which was some little way below, the well only partly full of water. In this case, however, he had to appeal to the woman to wind up the rope. And men say it was when this news was told to the other woman that her soul walked over the border line of treason.

Such, at least, were the stories told of him in the countryside, and there were many more—as that he had stood insolently in a splendid green dressing gown on the steps of a great hotel, and then led the police a chase through a long suite of grand apartments, and finally through his own bedroom on to a balcony that overhung the river. The moment the pursuers stepped on to the balcony it broke under them, and they dropped pell-mell into the eddying waters, while Michael, who had thrown off his gown and dived, was able to swim away. It was said that he had carefully cut away the props so that they would not support anything so heavy as a policeman. But here again he was immediately fortunate, yet ultimately unfortunate, for it is said that one of the men was drowned, leaving a family feud which made a little rift in his popularity. These stories can now be told in some detail, not because they are the most marvelous of his many adventures, but because these alone were not covered with silence by the loyalty of the peasantry. These alone found their way into official reports, and it is these which three of the chief officials of the country were reading and discussing when the more remarkable part of this story begins.

Night was far advanced and the lights shone in the cottage that served for a temporary police station near the coast. On one side of it were the last houses of the straggling village, and on the other nothing but a waste moorland stretching away toward the sea, the line of which was broken by no landmark except a solitary tower of the prehistoric pattern still found in Ireland, standing up as slender as a column, but pointed like a pyramid. At a wooden table in front of the window, which normally looked out on this landscape, sat two men in plain clothes, but with something of a military bearing, for indeed they were the two chiefs of the detective service of that district. The senior of the two, both in age and rank, was a sturdy man with a short white beard, and frosty eyebrows fixed in a frown which suggested rather worry than severity.

His name was Morton, and he was a Liverpool man long pickled in the Irish quarrels, and doing his duty among them in a sour fashion not altogether unsympathetic. He had spoken a few sentences to his companion, Nolan, a tall, dark man with a cadaverous equine Irish face, when he seemed to remember something and touched a bell which rang in another room. The subordinate he had summoned immediately appeared with a sheaf of papers in his hand.

"Sit down, Wilson," he said. "Those are the depositions, I suppose."

"Yes," replied the third officer. "I think I've got all there is to be got out of them, so I sent the people away."

"Did Mary Cregan give evidence?" asked Morton, with a frown that looked a little heavier than usual.

"No, but her master did," answered the man called Wilson, who had flat, red hair and a plain, pale face, not without sharpness. "I think he's hanging round the girl himself and is out against a rival. There's always some reason of that sort when we are told the truth about anything. And you bet the other girl told right enough."

"Well, let's hope they'll be some sort of use," remarked Nolan, in a somewhat hopeless manner, gazing out into the darkness.

"Anything is to the good," said Morton, "that lets us know anything about him."

"Do we know anything about him?" asked the melancholy Irishman.

"We know one thing about him," said Wilson, "and it's the one thing that nobody ever knew before. We know where he is."

"Are you sure?" inquired Morton, looking at him sharply.

"Quite sure," replied his assistant. "At this very minute he is in that tower over there by the shore. If you go near enough you'll see the candle burning in the window."

As he spoke the noise of a horn sounded on the road outside, and a moment after they heard the throbbing of a motor car brought to a standstill before the door. Morton instantly sprang to his feet.

"Thank the Lord that's the car from Dublin," he said. "I can't do anything without special authority, not if he were sitting on the top of the tower and putting out his tongue at us. But the chief can do what he thinks best."

He hurried out to the entrance and was soon exchanging greetings with a big handsome man in a fur coat, who brought into the dingy little station the indescribable glow of the great cities and the luxuries of the great world.

For this was Sir Walter Carey, an official of such eminence in Dublin Castle that nothing short of the case of Prince Michael would have brought him on such a journey in the middle of the night. But the case of Prince Michael, as it happened, was complicated by legalism as well as lawlessness. On the last occasion he had escaped by a forensic quibble and not, as usual, by a private escapade; and it was a question whether at the moment he was amenable to the law or not. It might be necessary to stretch a point, but a man like Sir Walter could probably stretch it as far as he liked.

Whether he intended to do so was a question to be considered. Despite the almost aggressive touch of luxury in the fur coat, it soon became apparent that Sir Walter's large leonine head was for use as well as ornament, and he considered the matter soberly and sanely enough. Five chairs were set round the plain deal table, for who should Sir Walter bring with him but his young relative and secretary, Horne Fisher. Sir Walter listened with grave attention, and his secretary with polite boredom, to the string of episodes by which the police had traced the flying rebel from the steps of the hotel to the solitary tower beside the sea. There at least he was cornered between the moors and the breakers; and the scout sent by Wilson reported him as writing under a solitary candle, perhaps composing another of his tremendous proclamations. Indeed, it would have been typical of him to choose it as the place in which finally to turn to bay. He had some remote claim on it, as on a family castle; and those who knew him thought him capable of imitating the primitive Irish chieftains who fell fighting against the sea.

"I saw some queer-looking people leaving as I came in," said Sir Walter Carey. "I suppose they were your witnesses. But why do they turn up here at this time of night?"

Morton smiled grimly. "They come here by night because they would be dead men if they came here by day. They are criminals committing a crime that is more horrible here than theft or murder."

"What crime do you mean?" asked the other, with some curiosity.

"They are helping the law," said Morton.

There was a silence, and Sir Walter considered the papers before him with an abstracted eye. At last he spoke.

"Quite so; but look here, if the local feeling is as lively as that there are a good many points to consider. I believe the new Act will enable me to collar him now if I think it best. But is it best? A serious rising would do us no good in Parliament, and the government has enemies in England as well as Ireland. It won't do if I have done what looks a little like sharp practice, and then only raised a revolution."

"It's all the other way," said the man called Wilson, rather quickly. "There won't be half so much of a revolution if you arrest him as there will if you leave him loose for three days longer. But, anyhow, there can't be anything nowadays that the proper police can't manage."

"Mr. Wilson is a Londoner," said the Irish detective, with a smile.

"Yes, I'm a cockney, all right," replied Wilson, "and I think I'm all the better for that. Especially at this job, oddly enough."

Sir Walter seemed slightly amused at the pertinacity of the third officer, and perhaps even more amused at the slight accent with which he spoke, which rendered rather needless his boast about his origin.

"Do you mean to say," he asked, "that you know more about the business here because you have come from London?"

"Sounds funny, I know, but I do believe it," answered Wilson. "I believe these affairs want fresh methods. But most of all I believe they want a fresh eye."

The superior officers laughed, and the redhaired man went on with a slight touch of temper:

"Well, look at the facts. See how the fellow got away every time, and you'll understand what I mean. Why was he able to stand in the place of the scarecrow, hidden by nothing but an old hat? Because it was a village policeman who knew the scarecrow was there, was expecting it, and therefore took no notice of it. Now I never expect a scarecrow. I've never seen one in the street, and I stare at one when I see it in the field. It's a new thing to me and worth noticing. And it was just the same when he hid in the well. You are ready to find a well in a place like that; you look for a well, and so you don't see it. I don't look for it, and therefore I do look at it."

"It is certainly an idea," said Sir Walter, smiling, "but what about the balcony? Balconies are occasionally seen in London."

"But not rivers right under them, as if it was in Venice," replied

Wilson.

"It is certainly a new idea," repeated Sir Walter, with something like respect. He had all the love of the luxurious classes for new ideas. But he also had a critical faculty, and was inclined to think, after due reflection, that it was a true idea as well.

Growing dawn had already turned the window panes from black to gray when Sir Walter got abruptly to his feet. The others rose also, taking this for a signal that the arrest was to be undertaken. But their leader stood for a moment in deep thought, as if conscious that he had come to a parting of the ways.

Suddenly the silence was pierced by a long, wailing cry from the dark moors outside. The silence that followed it seemed more startling than the shriek itself, and it lasted until Nolan said, heavily:

"'Tis the banshee. Somebody is marked for the grave."

His long, large-featured face was as pale as a moon, and it was easy to remember that he was the only Irishman in the room.

"Well, I know that banshee," said Wilson, cheerfully, "ignorant as you think I am of these things. I talked to that banshee myself an hour ago, and I sent that banshee up to the tower and told her to sing out like that if she could get a glimpse of our friend writing his proclamation."

"Do you mean that girl Bridget Royce?" asked Morton, drawing his frosty brows together. "Has she turned king's evidence to that extent?"

"Yes," answered Wilson. "I know very little of these local things, you tell me, but I reckon an angry woman is much the same in all countries."

Nolan, however, seemed still moody and unlike himself. "It's an ugly noise and an ugly business altogether," he said. "If it's really the end of Prince Michael it may well be the end of other things as well. When the spirit is on him he would escape by a ladder of dead men, and wade through that sea if it were made of blood."

"Is that the real reason of your pious alarms?" asked Wilson, with a slight sneer.

The Irishman's pale face blackened with a new passion.

"I have faced as many murderers in County Clare as you ever fought with in Clapham Junction, Mr. Cockney," he said.

"Hush, please," said Morton, sharply. "Wilson, you have no kind of right to imply doubt of your superior's conduct. I hope you will prove yourself as courageous and trustworthy as he has always been."

The pale face of the red-haired man seemed a shade paler, but he was silent and composed, and Sir Walter went up to Nolan with marked courtesy, saying, "Shall we go outside now, and get this business done?"

Dawn had lifted, leaving a wide chasm of white between a great gray cloud and the great gray moorland, beyond which the tower was outlined against the daybreak and the sea.

Something in its plain and primitive shape vaguely suggested the dawn in the first days of the earth, in some prehistoric time when even the colors were hardly created, when there was only blank daylight between cloud and clay. These dead hues were relieved only by one spot of gold—the spark of the candle alight in the window of the lonely tower, and burning on into the broadening daylight. As the group of detectives, followed by a cordon of policemen, spread out into a crescent to cut off all escape, the light in the tower flashed as if it were moved for a moment, and then went out. They knew the man inside had realized the daylight and blown out his candle.

"There are other windows, aren't there?" asked Morton, "and a door, of course, somewhere round the corner? Only a round tower has no corners."

"Another example of my small suggestion," observed Wilson, quietly. "That queer tower was the first thing I saw when I came to these parts; and I can tell you a little more about it—or, at any rate, the outside of it. There are four windows altogether, one a little way from this one, but just out of sight. Those are both on the ground floor, and so is the third on the other side, making a sort of triangle. But the fourth is just above the third, and I suppose it looks on an upper floor."

"It's only a sort of loft, reached by a ladder, said Nolan. "I've played in the place when I was a child. It's no more than an empty shell." And his sad face grew sadder, thinking perhaps of the tragedy of his country and the part that he played in it.

"The man must have got a table and chair, at any rate," said Wilson, "but no doubt he could have got those from some cottage. If I might make a suggestion, sir, I think we ought to approach all the five entrances at once, so to speak. One of us should go to the door and one to each window; Macbride here has a ladder for the upper window."

Mr. Horne Fisher languidly turned to his distinguished relative and spoke for the first time.

"I am rather a convert to the cockney school of psychology," he said in an almost inaudible voice.

The others seemed to feel the same influence in different ways, for the group began to break up in the manner indicated. Morton moved toward the window immediately in front of them, where the hidden outlaw had just snuffed the candle; Nolan, a little farther westward to the next window; while Wilson, followed by Macbride with the ladder, went round to the two windows at the back. Sir Walter Carey himself, followed by his secretary, began to walk round toward the only door, to demand admittance in a more regular fashion.

"He will be armed, of course," remarked Sir Walter, casually.

"By all accounts," replied Horne Fisher, "he can do more with a candlestick than most men with a pistol. But he is pretty sure to have the pistol, too."

Even as he spoke the question was answered with a tongue of thunder. Morton had just placed himself in front of the nearest window, his broad shoulders blocking the aperture. For an instant it was lit from within as with red fire, followed by a thundering throng of echoes. The square shoulders seemed to alter in shape, and the sturdy figure collapsed among the tall, rank grasses at the foot of the tower. A puff of smoke floated from the window like a little cloud. The two men behind rushed to the spot and raised him, but he was dead.

Sir Walter straightened himself and called out something that was lost in another noise of firing; it was possible that the police were already avenging their comrade from the other side. Fisher had already raced round to the next window, and a new cry of astonishment from him brought his patron to the same spot. Nolan, the Irish policeman, had also fallen, sprawling all his great length in the grass, and it was red with his blood. He was still alive when they reached him, but there was death on his face, and he was only able to make a final gesture telling them that all was over; and, with a broken word and a heroic effort, motioning them on to where his other comrades were besieging the back of the tower. Stunned by these rapid and repeated shocks, the two men could only vaguely obey the gesture, and, finding their way to the other windows at the back, they discovered a scene equally startling, if less final and tragic. The other two officers were not dead or mortally wounded, but Macbride lay with a broken leg and his ladder on top of him, evidently thrown down from the top window of the tower; while Wilson lay on his face, quite still as if stunned, with his red head among the gray and silver of the sea holly. In him, however, the impotence was but momentary, for he began to move and rise as the others came round the tower.

"My God! it's like an explosion!" cried Sir Walter; and indeed it was the only word for this unearthly energy, by which one man had been able to deal death or destruction on three sides of the same small triangle at the same instant.

Wilson had already scrambled to his feet and with splendid energy flew again at the window, revolver in hand. He fired twice into the opening and then disappeared in his own smoke; but the thud of his feet and the shock of a falling chair told them that the intrepid Londoner had managed at last to leap into the room. Then followed a curious silence; and Sir Walter, walking to the window through the thinning smoke, looked into the hollow shell of the ancient tower. Except for Wilson, staring around him, there was nobody there.

The inside of the tower was a single empty room, with nothing but a plain wooden chair and a table on which were pens, ink and paper, and the candlestick. Halfway up the high wall there was a rude timber platform under the upper window, a small loft which was more like a large shelf. It was reached only by a ladder, and it seemed to be as bare as the bare walls. Wilson completed his survey of the place and then went and stared at the things on the table. Then he silently pointed with his lean forefinger at the open page of the large notebook. The writer had suddenly stopped writing, even in the middle of a word.

"I said it was like an explosion," said Sir Walter Carey at last. "And really the man himself seems to have suddenly exploded. But he has blown himself up somehow without touching the tower. He's burst more like a bubble than a bomb."

"He has touched more valuable things than the tower," said Wilson, gloomily.

There was a long silence, and then Sir Walter said, seriously: "Well, Mr. Wilson, I am not a detective, and these unhappy happenings have left you in charge of that branch of the business. We all lament the cause of this, but I should like to say that I myself have the strongest confidence in your capacity for carrying on the work. What do you think we should do next?"

Wilson seemed to rouse himself from his depression and acknowledged the speaker's words with a warmer civility than he had hitherto shown to anybody. He called in a few of the police to assist in routing out the interior, leaving the rest to spread themselves in a search party outside.

"I think," he said, "the first thing is to make quite sure about the inside of this place, as it was hardly physically possible for him to have got outside. I suppose poor Nolan would have brought in his banshee and said it was supernaturally possible. But I've got no use for disembodied spirits when I'm dealing with facts. And the facts before me are an empty tower with a ladder, a chair, and a table."

"The spiritualists," said Sir Walter, with a smile, "would say that spirits could find a great deal of use for a table."

"I dare say they could if the spirits were on the table—in a bottle," replied Wilson, with a curl of his pale lip. "The people round here, when they're all sodden up with Irish whisky, may believe in such things. I think they want a little education in this country."

Horne Fisher's heavy eyelids fluttered in a faint attempt to rise, as if he were tempted to a lazy protest against the contemptuous tone of the investigator.

"The Irish believe far too much in spirits to believe in spiritualism," he murmured. "They know too much about 'em. If you want a simple and childlike faith in any spirit that comes along you can get it in your favorite London."

"I don't want to get it anywhere," said Wilson, shortly. "I say I'm dealing with much simpler things than your simple faith, with a table and a chair and a ladder. Now what I want to say about them at the start is this. They are all three made roughly enough of plain wood. But the table and the chair are fairly new and comparatively clean. The ladder is covered with dust and there is a cobweb under the top rung of it. That means that he borrowed the first two quite recently from some cottage, as we supposed, but the ladder has been a long time in this rotten old dustbin. Probably it was part of the original furniture, an heirloom in this magnificent palace of the Irish kings."

Again Fisher looked at him under his eyelids, but seemed too sleepy to speak, and Wilson went on with his argument.

"Now it's quite clear that something very odd has just happened in this place. The chances are ten to one, it seems to me, that it had something specially to do with this place. Probably he came here because he could do it only here; it doesn't seem very inviting otherwise. But the man knew it of old; they say it belonged to his family, so that altogether, I think, everything points to something in the construction of the tower itself."

"Your reasoning seems to me excellent," said Sir Walter, who was listening attentively. "But what could it be?"

"You see now what I mean about the ladder," went on the detective; "it's the only old piece of furniture here and the first thing that caught that cockney eye of mine. But there is something else. That loft up there is a sort of lumber room without any lumber. So far as I can see, it's as empty as everything else; and, as things are, I don't see the use of the ladder leading to it. It seems to me, as I can't find anything unusual down here, that it might pay us to look up there."

He got briskly off the table on which he was sitting (for the only chair was allotted to Sir Walter) and ran rapidly up the ladder to the platform above. He was soon followed by the others, Mr. Fisher going last, however, with an appearance of considerable nonchalance.

At this stage, however, they were destined to disappointment; Wilson nosed in every corner like a terrier and examined the roof almost in the posture of a fly, but half an hour afterward they had to confess that they were still without a clew. Sir Walter's private secretary seemed more and more threatened with inappropriate slumber, and, having been the last to climb up the ladder, seemed now to lack the energy even to climb down again.

"Come along, Fisher," called out Sir Walter from below, when the others had regained the floor. "We must consider whether we'll pull the whole place to pieces to see what it's made of."

"I'm coming in a minute," said the voice from the ledge above their heads, a voice somewhat suggestive of an articulate yawn.

"What are you waiting for?" asked Sir Walter, impatiently. "Can you see anything there?"

"Well, yes, in a way," replied the voice, vaguely. "In fact, I see it quite plain now."

"What is it?" asked Wilson, sharply, from the table on which he sat kicking his heels restlessly.

"Well, it's a man," said Horne Fisher.

Wilson bounded off the table as if he had been kicked off it. "What do you mean?" he cried. "How can you possibly see a man?"

"I can see him through the window," replied the secretary, mildly. "I see him coming across the moor. He's making a bee line across the open country toward this tower. He evidently means to pay us a visit. And, considering who it seems to be, perhaps it would be more polite if we were all at the door to receive him." And in a leisurely manner the secretary came down the ladder.

"Who it seems to be!" repeated Sir Walter in astonishment.

"Well, I think it's the man you call Prince Michael," observed Mr. Fisher, airily. "In fact, I'm sure it is. I've seen the police portraits of him."

There was a dead silence, and Sir Walter's usually steady brain seemed to go round like a windmill.

"But, hang it all!" he said at last, "even supposing his own explosion could have thrown him half a mile away, without passing through any of the windows, and left him alive enough for a country walk—even then, why the devil should he walk in this direction? The murderer does not generally revisit the scene of his crime so rapidly as all that."

"He doesn't know yet that it is the scene of his crime," answered

Horne Fisher.

"What on earth do you mean? You credit him with rather singular absence of mind."

"Well, the truth is, it isn't the scene of his crime," said Fisher, and went and looked out of the window.

There was another silence, and then Sir Walter said, quietly: "What sort of notion have you really got in your head, Fisher? Have you developed a new theory about how this fellow escaped out of the ring round him?"

"He never escaped at all," answered the man at the window, without turning round. "He never escaped out of the ring because he was never inside the ring. He was not in this tower at all, at least not when we were surrounding it."

He turned and leaned back against the window, but, in spite of his usual listless manner, they almost fancied that the face in shadow was a little pale.

"I began to guess something of the sort when we were some way from the tower," he said. "Did you notice that sort of flash or flicker the candle gave before it was extinguished? I was almost certain it was only the last leap the flame gives when a candle burns itself out. And then I came into this room and I saw that."

He pointed at the table and Sir Walter caught his breath with a sort of curse at his own blindness. For the candle in the candlestick had obviously burned itself away to nothing and left him, mentally, at least, very completely in the dark.

"Then there is a sort of mathematical question," went on Fisher, leaning back in his limp way and looking up at the bare walls, as if tracing imaginary diagrams there. "It's not so easy for a man in the third angle to face the other two at the same moment, especially if they are at the base of an isosceles. I am sorry if it sounds like a lecture on geometry, but—"

"I'm afraid we have no time for it," said Wilson, coldly. "If this man is really coming back, I must give my orders at once."

"I think I'll go on with it, though," observed Fisher, staring at the roof with insolent serenity.

"I must ask you, Mr. Fisher, to let me conduct my inquiry on my own lines," said Wilson, firmly. "I am the officer in charge now."

"Yes," remarked Horne Fisher, softly, but with an accent that somehow chilled the hearer. "Yes. But why?"

Sir Walter was staring, for he had never seen his rather lackadaisical young friend look like that before. Fisher was looking at Wilson with lifted lids, and the eyes under them seemed to have shed or shifted a film, as do the eyes of an eagle.

"Why are you the officer in charge now?" he asked. "Why can you conduct the inquiry on your own lines now? How did it come about, I wonder, that the elder officers are not here to interfere with anything you do?"

Nobody spoke, and nobody can say how soon anyone would have collected his wits to speak when a noise came from without. It was the heavy and hollow sound of a blow upon the door of the tower, and to their shaken spirits it sounded strangely like the hammer of doom.

The wooden door of the tower moved on its rusty hinges under the hand that struck it and Prince Michael came into the room. Nobody had the smallest doubt about his identity. His light clothes, though frayed with his adventures, were of fine and almost foppish cut, and he wore a pointed beard, or imperial, perhaps as a further reminiscence of Louis Napoleon; but he was a much taller and more graceful man that his prototype. Before anyone could speak he had silenced everyone for an instant with a slight but splendid gesture of hospitality.

"Gentlemen," he said, "this is a poor place now, but you are heartily welcome."

Wilson was the first to recover, and he took a stride toward the newcomer.

"Michael O'Neill, I arrest you in the king's name for the murder of

Francis Morton and James Nolan. It is my duty to warn you—"

"No, no, Mr. Wilson," cried Fisher, suddenly. "You shall not commit a third murder."

Sir Walter Carey rose from his chair, which fell over with a crash behind him. "What does all this mean?" he called out in an authoritative manner.

"It means," said Fisher, "that this man, Hooker Wilson, as soon as he had put his head in at that window, killed his two comrades who had put their heads in at the other windows, by firing across the empty room. That is what it means. And if you want to know, count how many times he is supposed to have fired and then count the charges left in his revolver."

Wilson, who was still sitting on the table, abruptly put a hand out for the weapon that lay beside him. But the next movement was the most unexpected of all, for the prince standing in the doorway passed suddenly from the dignity of a statue to the swiftness of an acrobat and rent the revolver out of the detective's hand.

"You dog!" he cried. "So you are the type of English truth, as I am of Irish tragedy—you who come to kill me, wading through the blood of your brethren. If they had fallen in a feud on the hillside, it would be called murder, and yet your sin might be forgiven you. But I, who am innocent, I was to be slain with ceremony. There would be long speeches and patient judges listening to my vain plea of innocence, noting down my despair and disregarding it. Yes, that is what I call assassination. But killing may be no murder; there is one shot left in this little gun, and I know where it should go."

Wilson turned quickly on the table, and even as he turned he twisted in agony, for Michael shot him through the body where he sat, so that he tumbled off the table like lumber.

The police rushed to lift him; Sir Walter stood speechless; and then, with a strange and weary gesture, Horne Fisher spoke.

"You are indeed a type of the Irish tragedy," he said. "You were entirely in the right, and you have put yourself in the wrong."

The prince's face was like marble for a space then there dawned in his eyes a light not unlike that of despair. He laughed suddenly and flung the smoking pistol on the ground.

"I am indeed in the wrong," he said. "I have committed a crime that may justly bring a curse on me and my children."

Horne Fisher did not seem entirely satisfied with this very sudden repentance; he kept his eyes on the man and only said, in a low voice, "What crime do you mean?"

"I have helped English justice," replied Prince Michael. "I have avenged your king's officers; I have done the work of his hangman. For that truly I deserve to be hanged."

And he turned to the police with a gesture that did not so much surrender to them, but rather command them to arrest him.

This was the story that Horne Fisher told to Harold March, the journalist, many years after, in a little, but luxurious, restaurant near Piccadilly. He had invited March to dinner some time after the affair he called "The Face in the Target," and the conversation had naturally turned on that mystery and afterward on earlier memories of Fisher's life and the way in which he was led to study such problems as those of Prince Michael. Horne Fisher was fifteen years older; his thin hair had faded to frontal baldness, and his long, thin hands dropped less with affectation and more with fatigue. And he told the story of the Irish adventure of his youth, because it recorded the first occasion on which he had ever come in contact with crime, or discovered how darkly and how terribly crime can be entangled with law.

"Hooker Wilson was the first criminal I ever knew, and he was a policeman," explained Fisher, twirling his wine glass. "And all my life has been a mixed-up business of the sort. He was a man of very real talent, and perhaps genius, and well worth studying, both as a detective and a criminal.

His white face and red hair were typical of him, for he was one of those who are cold and yet on fire for fame; and he could control anger, but not ambition. He swallowed the snubs of his superiors in that first quarrel, though he boiled with resentment; but when he suddenly saw the two heads dark against the dawn and framed in the two windows, he could not miss the chance, not only of revenge, but of the removal of the two obstacles to his promotion. He was a dead shot and counted on silencing both, though proof against him would have been hard in any case. But, as a matter of fact, he had a narrow escape, in the case of Nolan, who lived just long enough to say, 'Wilson' and point. We thought he was summoning help for his comrade, but he was really denouncing his murderer. After that it was easy to throw down the ladder above him (for a man up a ladder cannot see clearly what is below and behind) and to throw himself on the ground as another victim of the catastrophe.

"But there was mixed up with his murderous ambition a real belief, not only in his own talents, but in his own theories. He did believe in what he called a fresh eye, and he did want scope for fresh methods. There was something in his view, but it failed where such things commonly fail, because the fresh eye cannot see the unseen. It is true about the ladder and the scarecrow, but not about the life and the soul; and he made a bad mistake about what a man like Michael would do when he heard a woman scream. All Michael's very vanity and vainglory made him rush out at once; he would have walked into Dublin Castle for a lady's glove. Call it his pose or what you will, but he would have done it. What happened when he met her is another story, and one we may never know, but from tales I've heard since, they must have been reconciled. Wilson was wrong there; but there was something, for all that, in his notion that the newcomer sees most, and that the man on the spot may know too much to know anything. He was right about some things. He was right about me."

"About you?" asked Harold March in some wonder.

"I am the man who knows too much to know anything, or, at any rate, to do anything," said Horne Fisher. "I don't mean especially about Ireland. I mean about England. I mean about the whole way we are governed, and perhaps the only way we can be governed. You asked me just now what became of the survivors of that tragedy. Well, Wilson recovered and we managed to persuade him to retire. But we had to pension that damnable murderer more magnificently than any hero who ever fought for England. I managed to save Michael from the worst, but we had to send that perfectly innocent man to penal servitude for a crime we know he never committed, and it was only afterward that we could connive in a sneakish way at his escape. And Sir Walter Carey is Prime Minister of this country, which he would probably never have been if the truth had been told of such a horrible scandal in his department. It might have done for us altogether in Ireland; it would certainly have done for him. And he is my father's old friend, and has always smothered me with kindness. I am too tangled up with the whole thing, you see, and I was certainly never born to set it right. You look distressed, not to say shocked, and I'm not at all offended at it. Let us change the subject by all means, if you like. What do you think of this Burgundy? It's rather a discovery of mine, like the restaurant itself."

And he proceeded to talk learnedly and luxuriantly on all the wines of the world; on which subject, also, some moralists would consider that he knew too much.

III. THE SOUL OF THE SCHOOLBOY

A large map of London would be needed to display the wild and zigzag course of one day's journey undertaken by an uncle and his nephew; or, to speak more truly, of a nephew and his uncle. For the nephew, a schoolboy on a holiday, was in theory the god in the car, or in the cab, tram, tube, and so on, while his uncle was at most a priest dancing before him and offering sacrifices. To put it more soberly, the schoolboy had something of the stolid air of a young duke doing the grand tour, while his elderly relative was reduced to the position of a courier, who nevertheless had to pay for everything like a patron. The schoolboy was officially known as Summers Minor, and in a more social manner as Stinks, the only public tribute to his career as an amateur photographer and electrician. The uncle was the Rev. Thomas Twyford, a lean and lively old gentleman with a red, eager face and white hair. He was in the ordinary way a country clergyman, but he was one of those who achieve the paradox of being famous in an obscure way, because they are famous in an obscure world. In a small circle of ecclesiastical archaeologists, who were the only people who could even understand one another's discoveries, he occupied a recognized and respectable place. And a critic might have found even in that day's journey at least as much of the uncle's hobby as of the nephew's holiday.

His original purpose had been wholly paternal and festive. But, like many other intelligent people, he was not above the weakness of playing with a toy to amuse himself, on the theory that it would amuse a child. His toys were crowns and miters and croziers and swords of state; and he had lingered over them, telling himself that the boy ought to see all the sights of London. And at the end of the day, after a tremendous tea, he rather gave the game away by winding up with a visit in which hardly any human boy could be conceived as taking an interest—an underground chamber supposed to have been a chapel, recently excavated on the north bank of the Thames, and containing literally nothing whatever but one old silver coin. But the coin, to those who knew, was more solitary and splendid than the Koh-i-noor. It was Roman, and was said to bear the head of St. Paul; and round it raged the most vital controversies about the ancient British Church. It could hardly be denied, however, that the controversies left Summers Minor comparatively cold.

Indeed, the things that interested Summers Minor, and the things that did not interest him, had mystified and amused his uncle for several hours. He exhibited the English schoolboy's startling ignorance and startling knowledge —knowledge of some special classification in which he can generally correct and confound his elders. He considered himself entitled, at Hampton Court on a holiday, to forget the very names of Cardinal Wolsey or William of Orange; but he could hardly be dragged from some details about the arrangement of the electric bells in the neighboring hotel. He was solidly dazed by Westminster Abbey, which is not so unnatural since that church became the lumber room of the larger and less successful statuary of the eighteenth century. But he had a magic and minute knowledge of the Westminster omnibuses, and indeed of the whole omnibus system of London, the colors and numbers of which he knew as a herald knows heraldry. He would cry out against a momentary confusion between a light-green Paddington and a dark-green Bayswater vehicle, as his uncle would at the identification of a Greek ikon and a Roman image.

"Do you collect omnibuses like stamps?" asked his uncle. "They must need a rather large album. Or do you keep them in your locker?"

"I keep them in my head," replied the nephew, with legitimate firmness.

"It does you credit, I admit," replied the clergyman. "I suppose it were vain to ask for what purpose you have learned that out of a thousand things. There hardly seems to be a career in it, unless you could be permanently on the pavement to prevent old ladies getting into the wrong bus. Well, we must get out of this one, for this is our place. I want to show you what they call St. Paul's Penny."

"Is it like St. Paul's Cathedral?" asked the youth with resignation, as they alighted.

At the entrance their eyes were arrested by a singular figure evidently hovering there with a similar anxiety to enter. It was that of a dark, thin man in a long black robe rather like a cassock; but the black cap on his head was of too strange a shape to be a biretta. It suggested, rather, some archaic headdress of Persia or Babylon. He had a curious black beard appearing only at the corners of his chin, and his large eyes were oddly set in his face like the flat decorative eyes painted in old Egyptian profiles. Before they had gathered more than a general impression of him, he had dived into the doorway that was their own destination.

Nothing could be seen above ground of the sunken sanctuary except a strong wooden hut, of the sort recently run up for many military and official purposes, the wooden floor of which was indeed a mere platform over the excavated cavity below. A soldier stood as a sentry outside, and a superior soldier, an Anglo-Indian officer of distinction, sat writing at the desk inside. Indeed, the sightseers soon found that this particular sight was surrounded with the most extraordinary precautions. I have compared the silver coin to the Koh-i-noor, and in one sense it was even conventionally comparable, since by a historical accident it was at one time almost counted among the Crown jewels, or at least the Crown relics, until one of the royal princes publicly restored it to the shrine to which it was supposed to belong. Other causes combined to concentrate official vigilance upon it; there had been a scare about spies carrying explosives in small objects, and one of those experimental orders which pass like waves over bureaucracy had decreed first that all visitors should change their clothes for a sort of official sackcloth, and then (when this method caused some murmurs) that they should at least turn out their pockets. Colonel Morris, the officer in charge, was a short, active man with a grim and leathery face, but a lively and humorous eye—a contradiction borne out by his conduct, for he at once derided the safeguards and yet insisted on them.

"I don't care a button myself for Paul's Penny, or such things," he admitted in answer to some antiquarian openings from the clergyman who was slightly acquainted with him, "but I wear the King's coat, you know, and it's a serious thing when the King's uncle leaves a thing here with his own hands under my charge. But as for saints and relics and things, I fear I'm a bit of a Voltairian; what you would call a skeptic."

"I'm not sure it's even skeptical to believe in the royal family and not in the 'Holy' Family," replied Mr. Twyford. "But, of course, I can easily empty my pockets, to show I don't carry a bomb."

The little heap of the parson's possessions which he left on the table consisted chiefly of papers, over and above a pipe and a tobacco pouch and some Roman and Saxon coins. The rest were catalogues of old books, and pamphlets, like one entitled "The Use of Sarum," one glance at which was sufficient both for the colonel and the schoolboy. They could not see the use of Sarum at all. The contents of the boy's pockets naturally made a larger heap, and included marbles, a ball of string, an electric torch, a magnet, a small catapult, and, of course, a large pocketknife, almost to be described as a small tool box, a complex apparatus on which he seemed disposed to linger, pointing out that it included a pair of nippers, a tool for punching holes in wood, and, above all, an instrument for taking stones out of a horse's hoof. The comparative absence of any horse he appeared to regard as irrelevant, as if it were a mere appendage easily supplied. But when the turn came of the gentleman in the black gown, he did not turn out his pockets, but merely spread out his hands.

"I have no possessions," he said.

"I'm afraid I must ask you to empty your pockets and make sure," observed the colonel, gruffly.

"I have no pockets," said the stranger.

Mr. Twyford was looking at the long black gown with a learned eye.

"Are you a monk?" he asked, in a puzzled fashion.

"I am a magus," replied the stranger. "You have heard of the magi, perhaps? I am a magician."

"Oh, I say!" exclaimed Summers Minor, with prominent eyes.

"But I was once a monk," went on the other. "I am what you would call an escaped monk. Yes, I have escaped into eternity. But the monks held one truth at least, that the highest life should be without possessions. I have no pocket money and no pockets, and all the stars are my trinkets."

"They are out of reach, anyhow," observed Colonel Morris, in a tone which suggested that it was well for them. "I've known a good many magicians myself in India—mango plant and all. But the Indian ones are all frauds, I'll swear. In fact, I had a good deal of fun showing them up. More fun than I have over this dreary job, anyhow. But here comes Mr. Symon, who will show you over the old cellar downstairs."

Mr. Symon, the official guardian and guide, was a young man, prematurely gray, with a grave mouth which contrasted curiously with a very small, dark mustache with waxed points, that seemed somehow, separate from it, as if a black fly had settled on his face. He spoke with the accent of Oxford and the permanent official, but in as dead a fashion as the most indifferent hired guide. They descended a dark stone staircase, at the floor of which Symon pressed a button and a door opened on a dark room, or, rather, a room which had an instant before been dark. For almost as the heavy iron door swung open an almost blinding blaze of electric lights filled the whole interior. The fitful enthusiasm of Stinks at once caught fire, and he eagerly asked if the lights and the door worked together.

"Yes, it's all one system," replied Symon. "It was all fitted up for the day His Royal Highness deposited the thing here. You see, it's locked up behind a glass case exactly as he left it."

A glance showed that the arrangements for guarding the treasure were indeed as strong as they were simple. A single pane of glass cut off one corner of the room, in an iron framework let into the rock walls and the wooden roof above; there was now no possibility of reopening the case without elaborate labor, except by breaking the glass, which would probably arouse the night watchman who was always within a few feet of it, even if he had fallen asleep. A close examination would have showed many more ingenious safeguards; but the eye of the Rev. Thomas Twyford, at least, was already riveted on what interested him much more—the dull silver disk which shone in the white light against a plain background of black velvet.

"St. Paul's Penny, said to commemorate the visit of St. Paul to Britain, was probably preserved in this chapel until the eighth century," Symon was saying in his clear but colorless voice. "In the ninth century it is supposed to have been carried away by the barbarians, and it reappears, after the conversion of the northern Goths, in the possession of the royal family of Gothland. His Royal Highness, the Duke of Gothland, retained it always in his own private custody, and when he decided to exhibit it to the public, placed it here with his own hand. It was immediately sealed up in such a manner—"

Unluckily at this point Summers Minor, whose attention had somewhat strayed from the religious wars of the ninth century, caught sight of a short length of wire appearing in a broken patch in the wall. He precipitated himself at it, calling out, "I say, does that connect?"

It was evident that it did connect, for no sooner had the boy given it a twitch than the whole room went black, as if they had all been struck blind, and an instant afterward they heard the dull crash of the closing door.

"Well, you've done it now," said Symon, in his tranquil fashion. Then after a pause he added, "I suppose they'll miss us sooner or later, and no doubt they can get it open; but it may take some little time."

There was a silence, and then the unconquerable Stinks observed:

"Rotten that I had to leave my electric torch."

"I think," said his uncle, with restraint, "that we are sufficiently convinced of your interest in electricity."

Then after a pause he remarked, more amiably: "I suppose if I regretted any of my own impedimenta, it would be the pipe. Though, as a matter of fact, it's not much fun smoking in the dark. Everything seems different in the dark."

"Everything is different in the dark," said a third voice, that of the man who called himself a magician. It was a very musical voice, and rather in contrast with his sinister and swarthy visage, which was now invisible.

"Perhaps you don't know how terrible a truth that is. All you see are pictures made by the sun, faces and furniture and flowers and trees. The things themselves may be quite strange to you. Something else may be standing now where you saw a table or a chair. The face of your friend may be quite different in the dark."

A short, indescribable noise broke the stillness. Twyford started for a second, and then said, sharply:

"Really, I don't think it's a suitable occasion for trying to frighten a child."

"Who's a child?" cried the indignant Summers, with a voice that had a crow, but also something of a crack in it. "And who's a funk, either? Not me."

"I will be silent, then," said the other voice out of the darkness.

"But silence also makes and unmakes."

The required silence remained unbroken for a long time until at last the clergyman said to Symon in a low voice:

"I suppose it's all right about air?"

"Oh, yes," replied the other aloud; "there's a fireplace and a chimney in the office just by the door."

A bound and the noise of a falling chair told them that the irrepressible rising generation had once more thrown itself across the room. They heard the ejaculation: "A chimney! Why, I'll be—" and the rest was lost in muffled, but exultant, cries.

The uncle called repeatedly and vainly, groped his way at last to the opening, and, peering up it, caught a glimpse of a disk of daylight, which seemed to suggest that the fugitive had vanished in safety. Making his way back to the group by the glass case, he fell over the fallen chair and took a moment to collect himself again. He had opened his mouth to speak to Symon, when he stopped, and suddenly found himself blinking in the full shock of the white light, and looking over the other man's shoulder, he saw that the door was standing open.

"So they've got at us at last," he observed to Symon.

The man in the black robe was leaning against the wall some yards away, with a smile carved on his face.

"Here comes Colonel Morris," went on Twyford, still speaking to Symon. "One of us will have to tell him how the light went out. Will you?"

But Symon still said nothing. He was standing as still as a statue, and looking steadily at the black velvet behind the glass screen. He was looking at the black velvet because there was nothing else to look at. St. Paul's Penny was gone.

Colonel Morris entered the room with two new visitors; presumably two new sightseers delayed by the accident. The foremost was a tall, fair, rather languid-looking man with a bald brow and a high-bridged nose; his companion was a younger man with light, curly hair and frank, and even innocent, eyes. Symon scarcely seemed to hear the newcomers; it seemed almost as if he had not realized that the return of the light revealed his brooding attitude. Then he started in a guilty fashion, and when he saw the elder of the two strangers, his pale face seemed to turn a shade paler.

"Why it's Horne Fisher!" and then after a pause he said in a low voice, "I'm in the devil of a hole, Fisher."

"There does seem a bit of a mystery to be cleared up," observed the gentleman so addressed.

"It will never be cleared up," said the pale Symon. "If anybody could clear it up, you could. But nobody could."

"I rather think I could," said another voice from outside the group, and they turned in surprise to realize that the man in the black robe had spoken again.

"You!" said the colonel, sharply. "And how do you propose to play the detective?"

"I do not propose to play the detective," answered the other, in a clear voice like a bell. "I propose to play the magician. One of the magicians you show up in India, Colonel."

No one spoke for a moment, and then Horne Fisher surprised everybody by saying, "Well, let's go upstairs, and this gentleman can have a try."

He stopped Symon, who had an automatic finger on the button, saying:

"No, leave all the lights on. It's a sort of safeguard."

"The thing can't be taken away now," said Symon, bitterly.

"It can be put back," replied Fisher.

Twyford had already run upstairs for news of his vanishing nephew, and he received news of him in a way that at once puzzled and reassured him. On the floor above lay one of those large paper darts which boys throw at each other when the schoolmaster is out of the room. It had evidently been thrown in at the window, and on being unfolded displayed a scrawl of bad handwriting which ran: "Dear Uncle; I am all right. Meet you at the hotel later on," and then the signature.

Insensibly comforted by this, the clergyman found his thoughts reverting voluntarily to his favorite relic, which came a good second in his sympathies to his favorite nephew, and before he knew where he was he found himself encircled by the group discussing its loss, and more or less carried away on the current of their excitement. But an undercurrent of query continued to run in his mind, as to what had really happened to the boy, and what was the boy's exact definition of being all right.

Meanwhile Horne Fisher had considerably puzzled everybody with his new tone and attitude. He had talked to the colonel about the military and mechanical arrangements, and displayed a remarkable knowledge both of the details of discipline and the technicalities of electricity. He had talked to the clergyman, and shown an equally surprising knowledge of the religious and historical interests involved in the relic. He had talked to the man who called himself a magician, and not only surprised but scandalized the company by an equally sympathetic familiarity with the most fantastic forms of Oriental occultism and psychic experiment. And in this last and least respectable line of inquiry he was evidently prepared to go farthest; he openly encouraged the magician, and was plainly prepared to follow the wildest ways of investigation in which that magus might lead him.

"How would you begin now?" he inquired, with an anxious politeness that reduced the colonel to a congestion of rage.

"It is all a question of a force; of establishing communications for a force," replied that adept, affably, ignoring some military mutterings about the police force. "It is what you in the West used to call animal magnetism, but it is much more than that. I had better not say how much more. As to setting about it, the usual method is to throw some susceptible person into a trance, which serves as a sort of bridge or cord of communication, by which the force beyond can give him, as it were, an electric shock, and awaken his higher senses. It opens the sleeping eye of the mind."

"I'm suspectible," said Fisher, either with simplicity or with a baffling irony. "Why not open my mind's eye for me? My friend Harold March here will tell you I sometimes see things, even in the dark."

"Nobody sees anything except in the dark," said the magician.

Heavy clouds of sunset were closing round the wooden hut, enormous clouds, of which only the corners could be seen in the little window, like purple horns and tails, almost as if some huge monsters were prowling round the place. But the purple was already deepening to dark gray; it would soon be night.

"Do not light the lamp," said the magus with quiet authority, arresting a movement in that direction. "I told you before that things happen only in the dark."

How such a topsy-turvy scene ever came to be tolerated in the colonel's office, of all places, was afterward a puzzle in the memory of many, including the colonel. They recalled it like a sort of nightmare, like something they could not control. Perhaps there was really a magnetism about the mesmerist; perhaps there was even more magnetism about the man mesmerized. Anyhow, the man was being mesmerized, for Horne Fisher had collapsed into a chair with his long limbs loose and sprawling and his eyes staring at vacancy; and the other man was mesmerizing him, making sweeping movements with his darkly draped arms as if with black wings. The colonel had passed the point of explosion, and he dimly realized that eccentric aristocrats are allowed their fling. He comforted himself with the knowledge that he had already sent for the police, who would break up any such masquerade, and with lighting a cigar, the red end of which, in the gathering darkness, glowed with protest.

"Yes, I see pockets," the man in the trance was saying. "I see many pockets, but they are all empty. No; I see one pocket that is not empty."

There was a faint stir in the stillness, and the magician said, "Can you see what is in the pocket?"

"Yes," answered the other; "there are two bright things. I think they are two bits of steel. One of the pieces of steel is bent or crooked."

"Have they been used in the removal of the relic from downstairs?"

"Yes."

There was another pause and the inquirer added, "Do you see anything of the relic itself?"

"I see something shining on the floor, like the shadow or the ghost of it. It is over there in the corner beyond the desk."

There was a movement of men turning and then a sudden stillness, as of their stiffening, for over in the corner on the wooden floor there was really a round spot of pale light. It was the only spot of light in the room. The cigar had gone out.

"It points the way," came the voice of the oracle. "The spirits are pointing the way to penitence, and urging the thief to restitution. I can see nothing more." His voice trailed off into a silence that lasted solidly for many minutes, like the long silence below when the theft had been committed. Then it was broken by the ring of metal on the floor, and the sound of something spinning and falling like a tossed halfpenny.

"Light the lamp!" cried Fisher in a loud and even jovial voice, leaping to his feet with far less languor than usual. "I must be going now, but I should like to see it before I go. Why, I came on purpose to see it."

The lamp was lit, and he did see it, for St. Paul's Penny was lying on the floor at his feet.

"Oh, as for that," explained Fisher, when he was entertaining March and Twyford at lunch about a month later, "I merely wanted to play with the magician at his own game."

"I thought you meant to catch him in his own trap," said Twyford. "I can't make head or tail of anything yet, but to my mind he was always the suspect. I don't think he was necessarily a thief in the vulgar sense. The police always seem to think that silver is stolen for the sake of silver, but a thing like that might well be stolen out of some religious mania. A runaway monk turned mystic might well want it for some mystical purpose."

"No," replied Fisher, "the runaway monk is not a thief. At any rate he is not the thief. And he's not altogether a liar, either. He said one true thing at least that night."

"And what was that?" inquired March.

"He said it was all magnetism. As a matter of fact, it was done by means of a magnet." Then, seeing they still looked puzzled, he added, "It was that toy magnet belonging to your nephew, Mr. Twyford."

"But I don't understand," objected March. "If it was done with the schoolboy's magnet, I suppose it was done by the schoolboy."

"Well," replied Fisher, reflectively, "it rather depends which schoolboy."

"What on earth do you mean?"

"The soul of a schoolboy is a curious thing," Fisher continued, in a meditative manner. "It can survive a great many things besides climbing out of a chimney. A man can grow gray in great campaigns, and still have the soul of a schoolboy. A man can return with a great reputation from India and be put in charge of a great public treasure, and still have the soul of a schoolboy, waiting to be awakened by an accident. And it is ten times more so when to the schoolboy you add the skeptic, who is generally a sort of stunted schoolboy. You said just now that things might be done by religious mania. Have you ever heard of irreligious mania? I assure you it exists very violently, especially in men who like showing up magicians in India. But here the skeptic had the temptation of showing up a much more tremendous sham nearer home."

A light came into Harold March's eyes as he suddenly saw, as if afar off, the wider implication of the suggestion. But Twyford was still wrestling with one problem at a time.

"Do you really mean," he said, "that Colonel Morris took the relic?"

"He was the only person who could use the magnet," replied Fisher. "In fact, your obliging nephew left him a number of things he could use. He had a ball of string, and an instrument for making a hole in the wooden floor—I made a little play with that hole in the floor in my trance, by the way; with the lights left on below, it shone like a new shilling." Twyford suddenly bounded on his chair. "But in that case," he cried, in a new and altered voice, "why then of course— You said a piece of steel—?"

"I said there were two pieces of steel," said Fisher. "The bent piece of steel was the boy's magnet. The other was the relic in the glass case."

"But that is silver," answered the archaeologist, in a voice now almost unrecognizable.

"Oh," replied Fisher, soothingly, "I dare say it was painted with silver a little."

There was a heavy silence, and at last Harold March said, "But where is the real relic?"

"Where it has been for five years," replied Horne Fisher, "in the possession of a mad millionaire named Vandam, in Nebraska. There was a playful little photograph about him in a society paper the other day, mentioning his delusion, and saying he was always being taken in about relics."

Harold March frowned at the tablecloth; then, after an interval, he said: "I think I understand your notion of how the thing was actually done; according to that, Morris just made a hole and fished it up with a magnet at the end of a string. Such a monkey trick looks like mere madness, but I suppose he was mad, partly with the boredom of watching over what he felt was a fraud, though he couldn't prove it. Then came a chance to prove it, to himself at least, and he had what he called 'fun' with it. Yes, I think I see a lot of details now. But it's just the whole thing that knocks me. How did it all come to be like that?"

Fisher was looking at him with level lids and an immovable manner.

"Every precaution was taken," he said. "The Duke carried the relic on his own person, and locked it up in the case with his own hands."

March was silent; but Twyford stammered. "I don't understand you.

You give me the creeps. Why don't you speak plainer?"

"If I spoke plainer you would understand me less," said Horne

Fisher.

"All the same I should try," said March, still without lifting his head.

"Oh, very well," replied Fisher, with a sigh; "the plain truth is, of course, that it's a bad business. Everybody knows it's a bad business who knows anything about it. But it's always happening, and in one way one can hardly blame them. They get stuck on to a foreign princess that's as stiff as a Dutch doll, and they have their fling. In this case it was a pretty big fling."

The face of the Rev. Thomas Twyford certainly suggested that he was a little out of his depth in the seas of truth, but as the other went on speaking vaguely the old gentleman's features sharpened and set.

"If it were some decent morganatic affair I wouldn't say; but he must have been a fool to throw away thousands on a woman like that. At the end it was sheer blackmail; but it's something that the old ass didn't get it out of the taxpayers. He could only get it out of the Yank, and there you are."

The Rev. Thomas Twyford had risen to his feet.

"Well, I'm glad my nephew had nothing to do with it," he said. "And if that's what the world is like, I hope he will never have anything to do with it."

"I hope not," answered Horne Fisher. "No one knows so well as I do that one can have far too much to do with it."

For Summers Minor had indeed nothing to do with it; and it is part of his higher significance that he has really nothing to do with the story, or with any such stories. The boy went like a bullet through the tangle of this tale of crooked politics and crazy mockery and came out on the other side, pursuing his own unspoiled purposes. From the top of the chimney he climbed he had caught sight of a new omnibus, whose color and name he had never known, as a naturalist might see a new bird or a botanist a new flower. And he had been sufficiently enraptured in rushing after it, and riding away upon that fairy ship.

IV. THE BOTTOMLESS WELL

In an oasis, or green island, in the red and yellow seas of sand that stretch beyond Europe toward the sunrise, there can be found a rather fantastic contrast, which is none the less typical of such a place, since international treaties have made it an outpost of the British occupation. The site is famous among archaeologists for something that is hardly a monument, but merely a hole in the ground. But it is a round shaft, like that of a well, and probably a part of some great irrigation works of remote and disputed date, perhaps more ancient than anything in that ancient land. There is a green fringe of palm and prickly pear round the black mouth of the well; but nothing of the upper masonry remains except two bulky and battered stones standing like the pillars of a gateway of nowhere, in which some of the more transcendental archaeologists, in certain moods at moonrise or sunset, think they can trace the faint lines of figures or features of more than Babylonian monstrosity; while the more rationalistic archaeologists, in the more rational hours of daylight, see nothing but two shapeless rocks. It may have been noticed, however, that all Englishmen are not archaeologists. Many of those assembled in such a place for official and military purposes have hobbies other than archaeology. And it is a solemn fact that the English in this Eastern exile have contrived to make a small golf links out of the green scrub and sand; with a comfortable clubhouse at one end of it and this primeval monument at the other. They did not actually use this archaic abyss as a bunker, because it was by tradition unfathomable, and even for practical purposes unfathomed. Any sporting projectile sent into it might be counted most literally as a lost ball. But they often sauntered round it in their interludes of talking and smoking cigarettes, and one of them had just come down from the clubhouse to find another gazing somewhat moodily into the well.

Both the Englishmen wore light clothes and white pith helmets and puggrees, but there, for the most part, their resemblance ended. And they both almost simultaneously said the same word, but they said it on two totally different notes of the voice.

"Have you heard the news?" asked the man from the club. "Splendid."

"Splendid," replied the man by the well. But the first man pronounced the word as a young man might say it about a woman, and the second as an old man might say it about the weather, not without sincerity, but certainly without fervor.

And in this the tone of the two men was sufficiently typical of them. The first, who was a certain Captain Boyle, was of a bold and boyish type, dark, and with a sort of native heat in his face that did not belong to the atmosphere of the East, but rather to the ardors and ambitions of the West. The other was an older man and certainly an older resident, a civilian official—Horne Fisher; and his drooping eyelids and drooping light mustache expressed all the paradox of the Englishman in the East. He was much too hot to be anything but cool.

Neither of them thought it necessary to mention what it was that was splendid. That would indeed have been superfluous conversation about something that everybody knew. The striking victory over a menacing combination of Turks and Arabs in the north, won by troops under the command of Lord Hastings, the veteran of so many striking victories, was already spread by the newspapers all over the Empire, let alone to this small garrison so near to the battlefield.

"Now, no other nation in the world could have done a thing like that," cried Captain Boyle, emphatically.

Horne Fisher was still looking silently into the well; a moment later he answered: "We certainly have the art of unmaking mistakes. That's where the poor old Prussians went wrong. They could only make mistakes and stick to them. There is really a certain talent in unmaking a mistake."

"What do you mean," asked Boyle, "what mistakes?"

"Well, everybody knows it looked like biting off more than he could chew," replied Horne Fisher. It was a peculiarity of Mr. Fisher that he always said that everybody knew things which about one person in two million was ever allowed to hear of. "And it was certainly jolly lucky that Travers turned up so well in the nick of time. Odd how often the right thing's been done for us by the second in command, even when a great man was first in command. Like Colborne at Waterloo."

"It ought to add a whole province to the Empire," observed the other.

"Well, I suppose the Zimmernes would have insisted on it as far as the canal," observed Fisher, thoughtfully, "though everybody knows adding provinces doesn't always pay much nowadays."

Captain Boyle frowned in a slightly puzzled fashion. Being cloudily conscious of never having heard of the Zimmernes in his life, he could only remark, stolidly:

"Well, one can't be a Little Englander."

Horne Fisher smiled, and he had a pleasant smile.

"Every man out here is a Little Englander," he said. "He wishes he were back in Little England."

"I don't know what you're talking about, I'm afraid," said the younger man, rather suspiciously. "One would think you didn't really admire Hastings or—or—anything."

"I admire him no end," replied Fisher. "He's by far the best man for this post; he understands the Moslems and can do anything with them. That's why I'm all against pushing Travers against him, merely because of this last affair."

"I really don't understand what you're driving at," said the other, frankly.

"Perhaps it isn't worth understanding," answered Fisher, lightly, "and, anyhow, we needn't talk politics. Do you know the Arab legend about that well?"

"I'm afraid I don't know much about Arab legends," said Boyle, rather stiffly.

"That's rather a mistake," replied Fisher, "especially from your point of view. Lord Hastings himself is an Arab legend. That is perhaps the very greatest thing he really is. If his reputation went it would weaken us all over Asia and Africa. Well, the story about that hole in the ground, that goes down nobody knows where, has always fascinated me, rather. It's Mohammedan in form now, but I shouldn't wonder if the tale is a long way older than Mohammed. It's all about somebody they call the Sultan Aladdin, not our friend of the lamp, of course, but rather like him in having to do with genii or giants or something of that sort. They say he commanded the giants to build him a sort of pagoda, rising higher and higher above all the stars. The Utmost for the Highest, as the people said when they built the Tower of Babel. But the builders of the Tower of Babel were quite modest and domestic people, like mice, compared with old Aladdin. They only wanted a tower that would reach heaven— a mere trifle. He wanted a tower that would pass heaven and rise above it, and go on rising for ever and ever. And Allah cast him down to earth with a thunderbolt, which sank into the earth, boring a hole deeper and deeper, till it made a well that was without a bottom as the tower was to have been without a top. And down that inverted tower of darkness the soul of the proud Sultan is falling forever and ever."

"What a queer chap you are," said Boyle. "You talk as if a fellow could believe those fables."

"Perhaps I believe the moral and not the fable," answered Fisher.

"But here comes Lady Hastings. You know her, I think."

The clubhouse on the golf links was used, of course, for many other purposes besides that of golf. It was the only social center of the garrison beside the strictly military headquarters; it had a billiard room and a bar, and even an excellent reference library for those officers who were so perverse as to take their profession seriously. Among these was the great general himself, whose head of silver and face of bronze, like that of a brazen eagle, were often to be found bent over the charts and folios of the library. The great Lord Hastings believed in science and study, as in other severe ideals of life, and had given much paternal advice on the point to young Boyle, whose appearances in that place of research were rather more intermittent. It was from one of these snatches of study that the young man had just come out through the glass doors of the library on to the golf links. But, above all, the club was so appointed as to serve the social conveniences of ladies at least as much as gentlemen, and Lady Hastings was able to play the queen in such a society almost as much as in her own ballroom. She was eminently calculated and, as some said, eminently inclined to play such a part. She was much younger than her husband, an attractive and sometimes dangerously attractive lady; and Mr. Horne Fisher looked after her a little sardonically as she swept away with the young soldier. Then his rather dreary eye strayed to the green and prickly growths round the well, growths of that curious cactus formation in which one thick leaf grows directly out of the other without stalk or twig. It gave his fanciful mind a sinister feeling of a blind growth without shape or purpose. A flower or shrub in the West grows to the blossom which is its crown, and is content. But this was as if hands could grow out of hands or legs grow out of legs in a nightmare. "Always adding a province to the Empire," he said, with a smile, and then added, more sadly, "but I doubt if I was right, after all!"

A strong but genial voice broke in on his meditations and he looked up and smiled, seeing the face of an old friend. The voice was, indeed, rather more genial than the face, which was at the first glance decidedly grim. It was a typically legal face, with angular jaws and heavy, grizzled eyebrows; and it belonged to an eminently legal character, though he was now attached in a semimilitary capacity to the police of that wild district. Cuthbert Grayne was perhaps more of a criminologist than either a lawyer or a policeman, but in his more barbarous surroundings he had proved successful in turning himself into a practical combination of all three. The discovery of a whole series of strange Oriental crimes stood to his credit. But as few people were acquainted with, or attracted to, such a hobby or branch of knowledge, his intellectual life was somewhat solitary. Among the few exceptions was Horne Fisher, who had a curious capacity for talking to almost anybody about almost anything.

"Studying botany, or is it archaeology?" inquired Grayne. "I shall never come to the end of your interests, Fisher. I should say that what you don't know isn't worth knowing."

"You are wrong," replied Fisher, with a very unusual abruptness, and even bitterness. "It's what I do know that isn't worth knowing. All the seamy side of things, all the secret reasons and rotten motives and bribery and blackmail they call politics. I needn't be so proud of having been down all these sewers that I should brag about it to the little boys in the street."

"What do you mean? What's the matter with you?" asked his friend.

"I never knew you taken like this before."

"I'm ashamed of myself," replied Fisher. "I've just been throwing cold water on the enthusiasms of a boy."

"Even that explanation is hardly exhaustive," observed the criminal expert.

"Damned newspaper nonsense the enthusiasms were, of course," continued Fisher, "but I ought to know that at that age illusions can be ideals. And they're better than the reality, anyhow. But there is one very ugly responsibility about jolting a young man out of the rut of the most rotten ideal."

"And what may that be?" inquired his friend.

"It's very apt to set him off with the same energy in a much worse direction," answered Fisher; "a pretty endless sort of direction, a bottomless pit as deep as the bottomless well."

Fisher did not see his friend until a fortnight later, when he found himself in the garden at the back of the clubhouse on the opposite side from the links, a garden heavily colored and scented with sweet semitropical plants in the glow of a desert sunset. Two other men were with him, the third being the now celebrated second in command, familiar to everybody as Tom Travers, a lean, dark man, who looked older than his years, with a furrow in his brow and something morose about the very shape of his black mustache. They had just been served with black coffee by the Arab now officiating as the temporary servant of the club, though he was a figure already familiar, and even famous, as the old servant of the general. He went by the name of Said, and was notable among other Semites for that unnatural length of his yellow face and height of his narrow forehead which is sometimes seen among them, and gave an irrational impression of something sinister, in spite of his agreeable smile.

"I never feel as if I could quite trust that fellow," said Grayne, when the man had gone away. "It's very unjust, I take it, for he was certainly devoted to Hastings, and saved his life, they say. But Arabs are often like that, loyal to one man. I can't help feeling he might cut anybody else's throat, and even do it treacherously."

"Well," said Travers, with a rather sour smile, "so long as he leaves Hastings alone the world won't mind much."

There was a rather embarrassing silence, full of memories of the great battle, and then Horne Fisher said, quietly:

"The newspapers aren't the world, Tom. Don't you worry about them.

Everybody in your world knows the truth well enough."

"I think we'd better not talk about the general just now," remarked

Grayne, "for he's just coming out of the club."

"He's not coming here," said Fisher. "He's only seeing his wife to the car."

As he spoke, indeed, the lady came out on the steps of the club, followed by her husband, who then went swiftly in front of her to open the garden gate. As he did so she turned back and spoke for a moment to a solitary man still sitting in a cane chair in the shadow of the doorway, the only man left in the deserted club save for the three that lingered in the garden. Fisher peered for a moment into the shadow, and saw that it was Captain Boyle.

The next moment, rather to their surprise, the general reappeared and, remounting the steps, spoke a word or two to Boyle in his turn. Then he signaled to Said, who hurried up with two cups of coffee, and the two men re-entered the club, each carrying his cup in his hand. The next moment a gleam of white light in the growing darkness showed that the electric lamps had been turned on in the library beyond.

"Coffee and scientific researches," said Travers, grimly. "All the luxuries of learning and theoretical research. Well, I must be going, for I have my work to do as well." And he got up rather stiffly, saluted his companions, and strode away into the dusk.

"I only hope Boyle is sticking to scientific researches," said Horne Fisher. "I'm not very comfortable about him myself. But let's talk about something else."

They talked about something else longer than they probably imagined, until the tropical night had come and a splendid moon painted the whole scene with silver; but before it was bright enough to see by Fisher had already noted that the lights in the library had been abruptly extinguished. He waited for the two men to come out by the garden entrance, but nobody came.

"They must have gone for a stroll on the links," he said.

"Very possibly," replied Grayne. "It's going to be a beautiful night."

A moment or two after he had spoken they heard a voice hailing them out of the shadow of the clubhouse, and were astonished to perceive Travers hurrying toward them, calling out as he came:

"I shall want your help, you fellows," he cried. "There's something pretty bad out on the links."

They found themselves plunging through the club smoking room and the library beyond, in complete darkness, mental as well as material. But Horne Fisher, in spite of his affectation of indifference, was a person of a curious and almost transcendental sensibility to atmospheres, and he already felt the presence of something more than an accident. He collided with a piece of furniture in the library, and almost shuddered with the shock, for the thing moved as he could never have fancied a piece of furniture moving. It seemed to move like a living thing, yielding and yet striking back. The next moment

Grayne had turned on the lights, and he saw he had only stumbled against one of the revolving bookstands that had swung round and struck him; but his involuntary recoil had revealed to him his own subconscious sense of something mysterious and monstrous. There were several of these revolving bookcases standing here and there about the library; on one of them stood the two cups of coffee, and on another a large open book. It was Budge's book on Egyptian hieroglyphics, with colored plates of strange birds and gods, and even as he rushed past, he was conscious of something odd about the fact that this, and not any work of military science, should be open in that place at that moment. He was even conscious of the gap in the well-lined bookshelf from which it had been taken, and it seemed almost to gape at him in an ugly fashion, like a gap in the teeth of some sinister face.

A run brought them in a few minutes to the other side of the ground in front of the bottomless well, and a few yards from it, in a moonlight almost as broad as daylight, they saw what they had come to see.

The great Lord Hastings lay prone on his face, in a posture in which there was a touch of something strange and stiff, with one elbow erect above his body, the arm being doubled, and his big, bony hand clutching the rank and ragged grass. A few feet away was Boyle, almost as motionless, but supported on his hands and knees, and staring at the body. It might have been no more than shock and accident; but there was something ungainly and unnatural about the quadrupedal posture and the gaping face. It was as if his reason had fled from him. Behind, there was nothing but the clear blue southern sky, and the beginning of the desert, except for the two great broken stones in front of the well. And it was in such a light and atmosphere that men could fancy they traced in them enormous and evil faces, looking down.

Horne Fisher stooped and touched the strong hand that was still clutching the grass, and it was as cold as a stone. He knelt by the body and was busy for a moment applying other tests; then he rose again, and said, with a sort of confident despair:

"Lord Hastings is dead."

There was a stony silence, and then Travers remarked, gruffly: "This is your department, Grayne; I will leave you to question Captain Boyle. I can make no sense of what he says."

Boyle had pulled himself together and risen to his feet, but his face still wore an awful expression, making it like a new mask or the face of another man.

"I was looking at the well," he said, "and when I turned he had fallen down."

Grayne's face was very dark. "As you say, this is my affair," he said. "I must first ask you to help me carry him to the library and let me examine things thoroughly."

When they had deposited the body in the library, Grayne turned to Fisher and said, in a voice that had recovered its fullness and confidence, "I am going to lock myself in and make a thorough examination first. I look to you to keep in touch with the others and make a preliminary examination of Boyle. I will talk to him later. And just telephone to headquarters for a policeman, and let him come here at once and stand by till I want him."

Without more words the great criminal investigator went into the lighted library, shutting the door behind him, and Fisher, without replying, turned and began to talk quietly to Travers. "It is curious," he said, "that the thing should happen just in front of that place."

"It would certainly be very curious," replied Travers, "if the place played any part in it."

"I think," replied Fisher, "that the part it didn't play is more curious still."

And with these apparently meaningless words he turned to the shaken Boyle and, taking his arm, began to walk him up and down in the moonlight, talking in low tones.

Dawn had begun to break abrupt and white when Cuthbert Grayne turned out the lights in the library and came out on to the links. Fisher was lounging about alone, in his listless fashion; but the police messenger for whom he had sent was standing at attention in the background.

"I sent Boyle off with Travers," observed Fisher, carelessly; "he'll look after him, and he'd better have some sleep, anyhow."

"Did you get anything out of him?" asked Grayne. "Did he tell you what he and Hastings were doing?"

"Yes," answered Fisher, "he gave me a pretty clear account, after all. He said that after Lady Hastings went off in the car the general asked him to take coffee with him in the library and look up a point about local antiquities. He himself was beginning to look for Budge's book in one of the revolving bookstands when the general found it in one of the bookshelves on the wall. After looking at some of the plates they went out, it would seem, rather abruptly, on to the links, and walked toward the old well; and while Boyle was looking into it he heard a thud behind him, and turned round to find the general lying as we found him. He himself dropped on his knees to examine the body, and then was paralyzed with a sort of terror and could not come nearer to it or touch it. But I think very little of that; people caught in a real shock of surprise are sometimes found in the queerest postures."

Grayne wore a grim smile of attention, and said, after a short silence:

"Well, he hasn't told you many lies. It's really a creditably clear and consistent account of what happened, with everything of importance left out."

"Have you discovered anything in there?" asked Fisher.

"I have discovered everything," answered Grayne.

Fisher maintained a somewhat gloomy silence, as the other resumed his explanation in quiet and assured tones.

"You were quite right, Fisher, when you said that young fellow was in danger of going down dark ways toward the pit. Whether or no, as you fancied, the jolt you gave to his view of the general had anything to do with it, he has not been treating the general well for some time. It's an unpleasant business, and I don't want to dwell on it; but it's pretty plain that his wife was not treating him well, either. I don't know how far it went, but it went as far as concealment, anyhow; for when Lady Hastings spoke to Boyle it was to tell him she had hidden a note in the Budge book in the library. The general overheard, or came somehow to know, and he went straight to the book and found it. He confronted Boyle with it, and they had a scene, of course. And Boyle was confronted with something else; he was confronted with an awful alternative, in which the life of one old man meant ruin and his death meant triumph and even happiness."

"Well," observed Fisher, at last, "I don't blame him for not telling you the woman's part of the story. But how do you know about the letter?"

"I found it on the general's body," answered Grayne, "but I found worse things than that. The body had stiffened in the way rather peculiar to poisons of a certain Asiatic sort. Then I examined the coffee cups, and I knew enough chemistry to find poison in the dregs of one of them. Now, the General went straight to the bookcase, leaving his cup of coffee on the bookstand in the middle of the room. While his back was turned, and Boyle was pretending to examine the bookstand, he was left alone with the coffee cup. The poison takes about ten minutes to act, and ten minutes' walk would bring them to the bottomless well."

"Yes," remarked Fisher, "and what about the bottomless well?"

"What has the bottomless well got to do with it?" asked his friend.

"It has nothing to do with it," replied Fisher. "That is what I find utterly confounding and incredible."

"And why should that particular hole in the ground have anything to do with it?"

"It is a particular hole in your case," said Fisher. "But I won't insist on that just now. By the way, there is another thing I ought to tell you. I said I sent Boyle away in charge of Travers. It would be just as true to say I sent Travers in charge of Boyle."

"You don't mean to say you suspect Tom Travers?" cried the other.

"He was a deal bitterer against the general than Boyle ever was," observed Horne Fisher, with a curious indifference.

"Man, you're not saying what you mean," cried Grayne. "I tell you I found the poison in one of the coffee cups."

"There was always Said, of course," added Fisher, "either for hatred or hire. We agreed he was capable of almost anything."

"And we agreed he was incapable of hurting his master," retorted

Grayne.

"Well, well," said Fisher, amiably, "I dare say you are right; but I should just like to have a look at the library and the coffee cups."

He passed inside, while Grayne turned to the policeman in attendance and handed him a scribbled note, to be telegraphed from headquarters. The man saluted and hurried off; and Grayne, following his friend into the library, found him beside the bookstand in the middle of the room, on which were the empty cups.

"This is where Boyle looked for Budge, or pretended to look for him, according to your account," he said.

As Fisher spoke he bent down in a half-crouching attitude, to look at the volumes in the low, revolving shelf, for the whole bookstand was not much higher than an ordinary table. The next moment he sprang up as if he had been stung.

"Oh, my God!" he cried.

Very few people, if any, had ever seen Mr. Horne Fisher behave as he behaved just then. He flashed a glance at the door, saw that the open window was nearer, went out of it with a flying leap, as if over a hurdle, and went racing across the turf, in the track of the disappearing policeman. Grayne, who stood staring after him, soon saw his tall, loose figure, returning, restored to all its normal limpness and air of leisure. He was fanning himself slowly with a piece of paper, the telegram he had so violently intercepted.

"Lucky I stopped that," he observed. "We must keep this affair as quiet as death. Hastings must die of apoplexy or heart disease."

"What on earth is the trouble?" demanded the other investigator.

"The trouble is," said Fisher, "that in a few days we should have had a very agreeable alternative—of hanging an innocent man or knocking the British Empire to hell."

"Do you mean to say," asked Grayne, "that this infernal crime is not to be punished?"

Fisher looked at him steadily.

"It is already punished," he said.

After a moment's pause he went on. "You reconstructed the crime with admirable skill, old chap, and nearly all you said was true. Two men with two coffee cups did go into the library and did put their cups on the bookstand and did go together to the well, and one of them was a murderer and had put poison in the other's cup. But it was not done while Boyle was looking at the revolving bookcase. He did look at it, though, searching for the Budge book with the note in it, but I fancy that Hastings had already moved it to the shelves on the wall. It was part of that grim game that he should find it first.

"Now, how does a man search a revolving bookcase? He does not generally hop all round it in a squatting attitude, like a frog. He simply gives it a touch and makes it revolve."

He was frowning at the floor as he spoke, and there was a light under his heavy lids that was not often seen there. The mysticism that was buried deep under all the cynicism of his experience was awake and moving in the depths. His voice took unexpected turns and inflections, almost as if two men were speaking.

"That was what Boyle did; he barely touched the thing, and it went round as easily as the world goes round. Yes, very much as the world goes round, for the hand that turned it was not his. God, who turns the wheel of all the stars, touched that wheel and brought it full circle, that His dreadful justice might return."

"I am beginning," said Grayne, slowly, "to have some hazy and horrible idea of what you mean."

"It is very simple," said Fisher, "when Boyle straightened himself from his stooping posture, something had happened which he had not noticed, which his enemy had not noticed, which nobody had noticed. The two coffee cups had exactly changed places."

The rocky face of Grayne seemed to have sustained a shock in silence; not a line of it altered, but his voice when it came was unexpectedly weakened.

"I see what you mean," he said, "and, as you say, the less said about it the better. It was not the lover who tried to get rid of the husband, but—the other thing. And a tale like that about a man like that would ruin us here. Had you any guess of this at the start?"

"The bottomless well, as I told you," answered Fisher, quietly; "that was what stumped me from the start. Not because it had anything to do with it, because it had nothing to do with it."

He paused a moment, as if choosing an approach, and then went on: "When a man knows his enemy will be dead in ten minutes, and takes him to the edge of an unfathomable pit, he means to throw his body into it. What else should he do? A born fool would have the sense to do it, and Boyle is not a born fool. Well, why did not Boyle do it? The more I thought of it the more I suspected there was some mistake in the murder, so to speak. Somebody had taken somebody there to throw him in, and yet he was not thrown in. I had already an ugly, unformed idea of some substitution or reversal of parts; then I stooped to turn the bookstand myself, by accident, and I instantly knew everything, for I saw the two cups revolve once more, like moons in the sky."

After a pause, Cuthbert Grayne said, "And what are we to say to the newspapers?"

"My friend, Harold March, is coming along from Cairo to-day," said Fisher. "He is a very brilliant and successful journalist. But for all that he's a thoroughly honorable man, so you must not tell him the truth."

Half an hour later Fisher was again walking to and fro in front of the clubhouse, with Captain Boyle, the latter by this time with a very buffeted and bewildered air; perhaps a sadder and a wiser man.

"What about me, then?" he was saying. "Am I cleared? Am I not going to be cleared?"

"I believe and hope," answered Fisher, "that you are not going to be suspected. But you are certainly not going to be cleared. There must be no suspicion against him, and therefore no suspicion against you. Any suspicion against him, let alone such a story against him, would knock us endways from Malta to Mandalay. He was a hero as well as a holy terror among the Moslems. Indeed, you might almost call him a Moslem hero in the English service. Of course he got on with them partly because of his own little dose of Eastern blood; he got it from his mother, the dancer from Damascus; everybody knows that."

"Oh," repeated Boyle, mechanically, staring at him with round eyes, "everybody knows that."

"I dare say there was a touch of it in his jealousy and ferocious vengeance," went on Fisher. "But, for all that, the crime would ruin us among the Arabs, all the more because it was something like a crime against hospitality. It's been hateful for you and it's pretty horrid for me. But there are some things that damned well can't be done, and while I'm alive that's one of them."

"What do you mean?" asked Boyle, glancing at him curiously. "Why should you, of all people, be so passionate about it?"

Horne Fisher looked at the young man with a baffling expression.

"I suppose," he said, "it's because I'm a Little Englander."

"I can never make out what you mean by that sort of thing," answered

Boyle, doubtfully.

"Do you think England is so little as all that?" said Fisher, with a warmth in his cold voice, "that it can't hold a man across a few thousand miles. You lectured me with a lot of ideal patriotism, my young friend; but it's practical patriotism now for you and me, and with no lies to help it. You talked as if everything always went right with us all over the world, in a triumphant crescendo culminating in Hastings. I tell you everything has gone wrong with us here, except Hastings. He was the one name we had left to conjure with, and that mustn't go as well, no, by God! It's bad enough that a gang of infernal Jews should plant us here, where there's no earthly English interest to serve, and all hell beating up against us, simply because Nosey Zimmern has lent money to half the Cabinet. It's bad enough that an old pawnbroker from Bagdad should make us fight his battles; we can't fight with our right hand cut off. Our one score was Hastings and his victory, which was really somebody else's victory. Tom Travers has to suffer, and so have you."

Then, after a moment's silence, he pointed toward the bottomless well and said, in a quieter tone:

"I told you that I didn't believe in the philosophy of the Tower of Aladdin. I don't believe in the Empire growing until it reaches the sky; I don't believe in the Union Jack going up and up eternally like the Tower. But if you think I am going to let the Union Jack go down and down eternally, like the bottomless well, down into the blackness of the bottomless pit, down in defeat and derision, amid the jeers of the very Jews who have sucked us dry—no I won't, and that's flat; not if the Chancellor were blackmailed by twenty millionaires with their gutter rags, not if the Prime Minister married twenty Yankee Jewesses, not if Woodville and Carstairs had shares in twenty swindling mines. If the thing is really tottering, God help it, it mustn't be we who tip it over."

Boyle was regarding him with a bewilderment that was almost fear, and had even a touch of distaste.

"Somehow," he said, "there seems to be something rather horrid about the things you know."

"There is," replied Horne Fisher. "I am not at all pleased with my small stock of knowledge and reflection. But as it is partly responsible for your not being hanged, I don't know that you need complain of it."

And, as if a little ashamed of his first boast, he turned and strolled away toward the bottomless well.

V. THE FAD OF THE FISHERMAN

A thing can sometimes be too extraordinary to be remembered. If it is clean out of the course of things, and has apparently no causes and no consequences, subsequent events do not recall it, and it remains only a subconscious thing, to be stirred by some accident long after. It drifts apart like a forgotten dream; and it was in the hour of many dreams, at daybreak and very soon after the end of dark, that such a strange sight was given to a man sculling a boat down a river in the West country. The man was awake; indeed, he considered himself rather wide awake, being the political journalist, Harold March, on his way to interview various political celebrities in their country seats. But the thing he saw was so inconsequent that it might have been imaginary. It simply slipped past his mind and was lost in later and utterly different events; nor did he even recover the memory till he had long afterward discovered the meaning.

Pale mists of morning lay on the fields and the rushes along one margin of the river; along the other side ran a wall of tawny brick almost overhanging the water. He had shipped his oars and was drifting for a moment with the stream, when he turned his head and saw that the monotony of the long brick wall was broken by a bridge; rather an elegant eighteenth-century sort of bridge with little columns of white stone turning gray. There had been floods and the river still stood very high, with dwarfish trees waist deep in it, and rather a narrow arc of white dawn gleamed under the curve of the bridge.

As his own boat went under the dark archway he saw another boat coming toward him, rowed by a man as solitary as himself. His posture prevented much being seen of him, but as he neared the bridge he stood up in the boat and turned round. He was already so close to the dark entry, however, that his whole figure was black against the morning light, and March could see nothing of his face except the end of two long whiskers or mustaches that gave something sinister to the silhouette, like horns in the wrong place. Even these details March would never have noticed but for what happened in the same instant. As the man came under the low bridge he made a leap at it and hung, with his legs dangling, letting the boat float away from under him. March had a momentary vision of two black kicking legs; then of one black kicking leg; and then of nothing except the eddying stream and the long perspective of the wall. But whenever he thought of it again, long afterward, when he understood the story in which it figured, it was always fixed in that one fantastic shape—as if those wild legs were a grotesque graven ornament of the bridge itself, in the manner of a gargoyle. At the moment he merely passed, staring, down the stream. He could see no flying figure on the bridge, so it must have already fled; but he was half conscious of some faint significance in the fact that among the trees round the bridgehead opposite the wall he saw a lamp-post; and, beside the lamp-post, the broad blue back of an unconscious policeman.

Even before reaching the shrine of his political pilgrimage he had many other things to think of besides the odd incident of the bridge; for the management of a boat by a solitary man was not always easy even on such a solitary stream. And indeed it was only by an unforeseen accident that he was solitary. The boat had been purchased and the whole expedition planned in conjunction with a friend, who had at the last moment been forced to alter all his arrangements. Harold March was to have traveled with his friend Horne Fisher on that inland voyage to Willowood Place, where the Prime Minister was a guest at the moment. More and more people were hearing of Harold March, for his striking political articles were opening to him the doors of larger and larger salons; but he had never met the Prime Minister yet. Scarcely anybody among the general public had ever heard of Horne Fisher; but he had known the Prime Minister all his life. For these reasons, had the two taken the projected journey together, March might have been slightly disposed to hasten it and Fisher vaguely content to lengthen it out. For Fisher was one of those people who are born knowing the Prime Minister. The knowledge seemed to have no very exhilarant effect, and in his case bore some resemblance to being born tired. But he was distinctly annoyed to receive, just as he was doing a little light packing of fishing tackle and cigars for the journey, a telegram from Willowood asking him to come down at once by train, as the Prime Minister had to leave that night. Fisher knew that his friend the journalist could not possibly start till the next day, and he liked his friend the journalist, and had looked forward to a few days on the river. He did not particularly like or dislike the Prime Minister, but he intensely disliked the alternative of a few hours in the train. Nevertheless, he accepted Prime Ministers as he accepted railway trains—as part of a system which he, at least, was not the revolutionist sent on earth to destroy. So he telephoned to March, asking him, with many apologetic curses and faint damns, to take the boat down the river as arranged, that they might meet at Willowood by the time settled; then he went outside and hailed a taxicab to take him to the railway station. There he paused at the bookstall to add to his light luggage a number of cheap murder stories, which he read with great pleasure, and without any premonition that he was about to walk into as strange a story in real life.

A little before sunset he arrived, with his light suitcase in hand, before the gate of the long riverside gardens of Willowood Place, one of the smaller seats of Sir Isaac Hook, the master of much shipping and many newspapers. He entered by the gate giving on the road, at the opposite side to the river, but there was a mixed quality in all that watery landscape which perpetually reminded a traveler that the river was near. White gleams of water would shine suddenly like swords or spears in the green thickets. And even in the garden itself, divided into courts and curtained with hedges and high garden trees, there hung everywhere in the air the music of water. The first of the green courts which he entered appeared to be a somewhat neglected croquet lawn, in which was a solitary young man playing croquet against himself. Yet he was not an enthusiast for the game, or even for the garden; and his sallow but well-featured face looked rather sullen than otherwise. He was only one of those young men who cannot support the burden of consciousness unless they are doing something, and whose conceptions of doing something are limited to a game of some kind. He was dark and well dressed in a light holiday fashion, and Fisher recognized him at once as a young man named James Bullen, called, for some unknown reason, Bunker. He was the nephew of Sir Isaac; but, what was much more important at the moment, he was also the private secretary of the Prime Minister.

"Hullo, Bunker!" observed Horne Fisher. "You're the sort of man I wanted to see. Has your chief come down yet?"

"He's only staying for dinner," replied Bullen, with his eye on the yellow ball. "He's got a great speech to-morrow at Birmingham and he's going straight through to-night. He's motoring himself there; driving the car, I mean. It's the one thing he's really proud of."

"You mean you're staying here with your uncle, like a good boy?" replied Fisher. "But what will the Chief do at Birmingham without the epigrams whispered to him by his brilliant secretary?"

"Don't you start ragging me," said the young man called Bunker. "I'm only too glad not to go trailing after him. He doesn't know a thing about maps or money or hotels or anything, and I have to dance about like a courier. As for my uncle, as I'm supposed to come into the estate, it's only decent to be here sometimes."

"Very proper," replied the other. "Well, I shall see you later on," and, crossing the lawn, he passed out through a gap in the hedge.

He was walking across the lawn toward the landing stage on the river, and still felt all around him, under the dome of golden evening, an Old World savor and reverberation in that riverhaunted garden. The next square of turf which he crossed seemed at first sight quite deserted, till he saw in the twilight of trees in one corner of it a hammock and in the hammock a man, reading a newspaper and swinging one leg over the edge of the net.

Him also he hailed by name, and the man slipped to the ground and strolled forward. It seemed fated that he should feel something of the past in the accidents of that place, for the figure might well have been an early-Victorian ghost revisiting the ghosts of the croquet hoops and mallets. It was the figure of an elderly man with long whiskers that looked almost fantastic, and a quaint and careful cut of collar and cravat. Having been a fashionable dandy forty years ago, he had managed to preserve the dandyism while ignoring the fashions. A white top-hat lay beside the Morning Post in the hammock behind him. This was the Duke of Westmoreland, the relic of a family really some centuries old; and the antiquity was not heraldry but history. Nobody knew better than Fisher how rare such noblemen are in fact, and how numerous in fiction. But whether the duke owed the general respect he enjoyed to the genuineness of his pedigree or to the fact that he owned a vast amount of very valuable property was a point about which Mr. Fisher's opinion might have been more interesting to discover.

"You were looking so comfortable," said Fisher, "that I thought you must be one of the servants. I'm looking for somebody to take this bag of mine; I haven't brought a man down, as I came away in a hurry."

"Nor have I, for that matter," replied the duke, with some pride. "I never do. If there's one animal alive I loathe it's a valet. I learned to dress myself at an early age and was supposed to do it decently. I may be in my second childhood, but I've not go so far as being dressed like a child."

"The Prime Minister hasn't brought a valet; he's brought a secretary instead," observed Fisher. "Devilish inferior job. Didn't I hear that Harker was down here?"

"He's over there on the landing stage," replied the duke, indifferently, and resumed the study of the Morning Post.

Fisher made his way beyond the last green wall of the garden on to a sort of towing path looking on the river and a wooden island opposite. There, indeed, he saw a lean, dark figure with a stoop almost like that of a vulture, a posture well known in the law courts as that of Sir John Harker, the Attorney-General. His face was lined with headwork, for alone among the three idlers in the garden he was a man who had made his own way; and round his bald brow and hollow temples clung dull red hair, quite flat, like plates of copper.

"I haven't seen my host yet," said Horne Fisher, in a slightly more serious tone than he had used to the others, "but I suppose I shall meet him at dinner."

"You can see him now; but you can't meet him," answered Harker.

He nodded his head toward one end of the island opposite, and, looking steadily in the same direction, the other guest could see the dome of a bald head and the top of a fishing rod, both equally motionless, rising out of the tall undergrowth against the background of the stream beyond. The fisherman seemed to be seated against the stump of a tree and facing toward the other bank, so that his face could not be seen, but the shape of his head was unmistakable.

"He doesn't like to be disturbed when he's fishing," continued Harker. "It's a sort of fad of his to eat nothing but fish, and he's very proud of catching his own. Of course he's all for simplicity, like so many of these millionaires. He likes to come in saying he's worked for his daily bread like a laborer."

"Does he explain how he blows all the glass and stuffs all the upholstery," asked Fisher, "and makes all the silver forks, and grows all the grapes and peaches, and designs all the patterns on the carpets? I've always heard he was a busy man."

"I don't think he mentioned it," answered the lawyer. "What is the meaning of this social satire?"

"Well, I am a trifle tired," said Fisher, "of the Simple Life and the Strenuous Life as lived by our little set. We're all really dependent in nearly everything, and we all make a fuss about being independent in something. The Prime Minister prides himself on doing without a chauffeur, but he can't do without a factotum and Jack-of-all-trades; and poor old Bunker has to play the part of a universal genius, which God knows he was never meant for. The duke prides himself on doing without a valet, but, for all that, he must give a lot of people an infernal lot of trouble to collect such extraordinary old clothes as he wears. He must have them looked up in the British Museum or excavated out of the tombs. That white hat alone must require a sort of expedition fitted out to find it, like the North Pole. And here we have old Hook pretending to produce his own fish when he couldn't produce his own fish knives or fish forks to eat it with. He may be simple about simple things like food, but you bet he's luxurious about luxurious things, especially little things. I don't include you; you've worked too hard to enjoy playing at work."

"I sometimes think," said Harker, "that you conceal a horrid secret of being useful sometimes. Haven't you come down here to see Number One before he goes on to Birmingham?"

Horne Fisher answered, in a lower voice: "Yes; and I hope to be lucky enough to catch him before dinner. He's got to see Sir Isaac about something just afterward."

"Hullo!" exclaimed Harker. "Sir Isaac's finished his fishing. I know he prides himself on getting up at sunrise and going in at sunset."

The old man on the island had indeed risen to his feet, facing round and showing a bush of gray beard with rather small, sunken features, but fierce eyebrows and keen, choleric eyes. Carefully carrying his fishing tackle, he was already making his way back to the mainland across a bridge of flat stepping-stones a little way down the shallow stream; then he veered round, coming toward his guests and civilly saluting them. There were several fish in his basket and he was in a good temper.

"Yes," he said, acknowledging Fisher's polite expression of surprise, "I get up before anybody else in the house, I think. The early bird catches the worm."

"Unfortunately," said Harker, "it is the early fish that catches the worm."

"But the early man catches the fish," replied the old man, gruffly.

"But from what I hear, Sir Isaac, you are the late man, too," interposed Fisher. "You must do with very little sleep."

"I never had much time for sleeping," answered Hook, "and I shall have to be the late man to-night, anyhow. The Prime Minister wants to have a talk, he tells me, and, all things considered, I think we'd better be dressing for dinner."

Dinner passed off that evening without a word of politics and little enough but ceremonial trifles. The Prime Minister, Lord Merivale, who was a long, slim man with curly gray hair, was gravely complimentary to his host about his success as a fisherman and the skill and patience he displayed; the conversation flowed like the shallow stream through the stepping-stones.

"It wants patience to wait for them, no doubt," said Sir Isaac, "and skill to play them, but I'm generally pretty lucky at it."

"Does a big fish ever break the line and get away?" inquired the politician, with respectful interest.

"Not the sort of line I use," answered Hook, with satisfaction. "I rather specialize in tackle, as a matter of fact. If he were strong enough to do that, he'd be strong enough to pull me into the river."

"A great loss to the community," said the Prime Minister, bowing.

Fisher had listened to all these futilities with inward impatience, waiting for his own opportunity, and when the host rose he sprang to his feet with an alertness he rarely showed. He managed to catch Lord Merivale before Sir Isaac bore him off for the final interview. He had only a few words to say, but he wanted to get them said.

He said, in a low voice as he opened the door for the Premier, "I have seen Montmirail; he says that unless we protest immediately on behalf of Denmark, Sweden will certainly seize the ports."

Lord Merivale nodded. "I'm just going to hear what Hook has to say about it," he said.

"I imagine," said Fisher, with a faint smile, "that there is very little doubt what he will say about it."

Merivale did not answer, but lounged gracefully toward the library, whither his host had already preceded him. The rest drifted toward the billiard room, Fisher merely remarking to the lawyer: "They won't be long. We know they're practically in agreement."

"Hook entirely supports the Prime Minister," assented Harker.

"Or the Prime Minister entirely supports Hook," said Horne Fisher, and began idly to knock the balls about on the billiard table.

Horne Fisher came down next morning in a late and leisurely fashion, as was his reprehensible habit; he had evidently no appetite for catching worms. But the other guests seemed to have felt a similar indifference, and they helped themselves to breakfast from the sideboard at intervals during the hours verging upon lunch. So that it was not many hours later when the first sensation of that strange day came upon them. It came in the form of a young man with light hair and a candid expression, who came sculling down the river and disembarked at the landing stage. It was, in fact, no other than Mr. Harold March, whose journey had begun far away up the river in the earliest hours of that day. He arrived late in the afternoon, having stopped for tea in a large riverside town, and he had a pink evening paper sticking out of his pocket. He fell on the riverside garden like a quiet and well-behaved thunderbolt, but he was a thunderbolt without knowing it.

The first exchange of salutations and introductions was commonplace enough, and consisted, indeed, of the inevitable repetition of excuses for the eccentric seclusion of the host. He had gone fishing again, of course, and must not be disturbed till the appointed hour, though he sat within a stone's throw of where they stood.

"You see it's his only hobby," observed Harker, apologetically, "and, after all, it's his own house; and he's very hospitable in other ways."

"I'm rather afraid," said Fisher, in a lower voice, "that it's becoming more of a mania than a hobby. I know how it is when a man of that age begins to collect things, if it's only collecting those rotten little river fish. You remember Talbot's uncle with his toothpicks, and poor old Buzzy and the waste of cigar ashes. Hook has done a lot of big things in his time—the great deal in the Swedish timber trade and the Peace Conference at Chicago—but I doubt whether he cares now for any of those big things as he cares for those little fish."

"Oh, come, come," protested the Attorney-General. "You'll make Mr. March think he has come to call on a lunatic. Believe me, Hook only does it for fun, like any other sport, only he's of the kind that takes his fun sadly. But I bet if there were big news about timber or shipping, he would drop his fun and his fish all right."

"Well, I wonder," said Horne Fisher, looking sleepily at the island in the river.

"By the way, is there any news of anything?" asked Harker of Harold March. "I see you've got an evening paper; one of those enterprising evening papers that come out in the morning."

"The beginning of Lord Merivale's Birmingham speech," replied March, handing him the paper. "It's only a paragraph, but it seems to me rather good."

Harker took the paper, flapped and refolded it, and looked at the "Stop Press" news. It was, as March had said, only a paragraph. But it was a paragraph that had a peculiar effect on Sir John Harker. His lowering brows lifted with a flicker and his eyes blinked, and for a moment his leathery jaw was loosened. He looked in some odd fashion like a very old man. Then, hardening his voice and handing the paper to Fisher without a tremor, he simply said:

"Well, here's a chance for the bet. You've got your big news to disturb the old man's fishing."

Horne Fisher was looking at the paper, and over his more languid and less expressive features a change also seemed to pass. Even that little paragraph had two or three large headlines, and his eye encountered, "Sensational Warning to Sweden," and, "We Shall Protest."

"What the devil—" he said, and his words softened first to a whisper and then a whistle.

"We must tell old Hook at once, or he'll never forgive us," said Harker.

"He'll probably want to see Number One instantly, though it may be too late now. I'm going across to him at once. I bet I'll make him forget his fish, anyhow." And, turning his back, he made his way hurriedly along the riverside to the causeway of flat stones.

March was staring at Fisher, in amazement at the effect his pink paper had produced.

"What does it all mean?" he cried. "I always supposed we should protest in defense of the Danish ports, for their sakes and our own. What is all this botheration about Sir Isaac and the rest of you? Do you think it bad news?"

"Bad news!" repeated Fisher, with a sort of soft emphasis beyond expression.

"Is it as bad as all that?" asked his friend, at last.

"As bad as all that?" repeated Fisher. "Why of course it's as good as it can be. It's great news. It's glorious news! That's where the devil of it comes in, to knock us all silly. It's admirable. It's inestimable. It is also quite incredible."

He gazed again at the gray and green colors of the island and the river, and his rather dreary eye traveled slowly round to the hedges and the lawns.

"I felt this garden was a sort of dream," he said, "and I suppose I must be dreaming. But there is grass growing and water moving; and something impossible has happened."

Even as he spoke the dark figure with a stoop like a vulture appeared in the gap of the hedge just above him.

"You have won your bet," said Harker, in a harsh and almost croaking voice. "The old fool cares for nothing but fishing. He cursed me and told me he would talk no politics."

"I thought it might be so," said Fisher, modestly. "What are you going to do next?"

"I shall use the old idiot's telephone, anyhow," replied the lawyer. "I must find out exactly what has happened. I've got to speak for the Government myself to-morrow." And he hurried away toward the house.

In the silence that followed, a very bewildering silence so far as March was concerned, they saw the quaint figure of the Duke of Westmoreland, with his white hat and whiskers, approaching them across the garden. Fisher instantly stepped toward him with the pink paper in his hand, and, with a few words, pointed out the apocalyptic paragraph. The duke, who had been walking slowly, stood quite still, and for some seconds he looked like a tailor's dummy standing and staring outside some antiquated shop. Then March heard his voice, and it was high and almost hysterical:

"But he must see it; he must be made to understand. It cannot have been put to him properly." Then, with a certain recovery of fullness and even pomposity in the voice, "I shall go and tell him myself."

Among the queer incidents of that afternoon, March always remembered something almost comical about the clear picture of the old gentleman in his wonderful white hat carefully stepping from stone to stone across the river, like a figure crossing the traffic in Piccadilly. Then he disappeared behind the trees of the island, and March and Fisher turned to meet the Attorney-General, who was coming out of the house with a visage of grim assurance.

"Everybody is saying," he said, "that the Prime Minister has made the greatest speech of his life. Peroration and loud and prolonged cheers. Corrupt financiers and heroic peasants. We will not desert Denmark again."

Fisher nodded and turned away toward the towing path, where he saw the duke returning with a rather dazed expression. In answer to questions he said, in a husky and confidential voice:

"I really think our poor friend cannot be himself. He refused to listen; he—ah—suggested that I might frighten the fish."

A keen ear might have detected a murmur from Mr. Fisher on the subject of a white hat, but Sir John Harker struck it more decisively:

"Fisher was quite right. I didn't believe it myself, but it's quite clear that the old fellow is fixed on this fishing notion by now. If the house caught fire behind him he would hardly move till sunset."

Fisher had continued his stroll toward the higher embanked ground of the towing path, and he now swept a long and searching gaze, not toward the island, but toward the distant wooded heights that were the walls of the valley. An evening sky as clear as that of the previous day was settling down all over the dim landscape, but toward the west it was now red rather than gold; there was scarcely any sound but the monotonous music of the river. Then came the sound of a half-stifled exclamation from Horne Fisher, and Harold March looked up at him in wonder.

"You spoke of bad news," said Fisher. "Well, there is really bad news now. I am afraid this is a bad business."

"What bad news do you mean?" asked his friend, conscious of something strange and sinister in his voice.

"The sun has set," answered Fisher.

He went on with the air of one conscious of having said something fatal.

"We must get somebody to go across whom he will really listen to. He may be mad, but there's method in his madness. There nearly always is method in madness. It's what drives men mad, being methodical. And he never goes on sitting there after sunset, with the whole place getting dark. Where's his nephew? I believe he's really fond of his nephew."

"Look!" cried March, abruptly. "Why, he's been across already.

There he is coming back."

And, looking up the river once more, they saw, dark against the sunset reflections, the figure of James Bullen stepping hastily and rather clumsily from stone to stone. Once he slipped on a stone with a slight splash. When he rejoined the group on the bank his olive face was unnaturally pale.

The other four men had already gathered on the same spot and almost simultaneously were calling out to him, "What does he say now?"

"Nothing. He says—nothing."

Fisher looked at the young man steadily for a moment; then he started from his immobility and, making a motion to March to follow him, himself strode down to the river crossing. In a few moments they were on the little beaten track that ran round the wooded island, to the other side of it where the fisherman sat. Then they stood and looked at him, without a word.

Sir Isaac Hook was still sitting propped up against the stump of the tree, and that for the best of reasons. A length of his own infallible fishing line was twisted and tightened twice round his throat and then twice round the wooden prop behind him. The leading investigator ran forward and touched the fisherman's hand, and it was as cold as a fish.

"The sun has set," said Horne Fisher, in the same terrible tones, "and he will never see it rise again."

Ten minutes afterward the five men, shaken by such a shock, were again together in the garden, looking at one another with white but watchful faces. The lawyer seemed the most alert of the group; he was articulate if somewhat abrupt.

"We must leave the body as it is and telephone for the police," he said. "I think my own authority will stretch to examining the servants and the poor fellow's papers, to see if there is anything that concerns them. Of course, none of you gentlemen must leave this place."

Perhaps there was something in his rapid and rigorous legality that suggested the closing of a net or trap. Anyhow, young Bullen suddenly broke down, or perhaps blew up, for his voice was like an explosion in the silent garden.

"I never touched him," he cried. "I swear I had nothing to do with it!"

"Who said you had?" demanded Harker, with a hard eye. "Why do you cry out before you're hurt?"

"Because you all look at me like that," cried the young man, angrily. "Do you think I don't know you're always talking about my damned debts and expectations?"

Rather to March's surprise, Fisher had drawn away from this first collision, leading the duke with him to another part of the garden. When he was out of earshot of the others he said, with a curious simplicity of manner:

"Westmoreland, I am going straight to the point."

"Well?" said the other, staring at him stolidly.

"You have a motive for killing him," said Fisher.

The duke continued to stare, but he seemed unable to speak.

"I hope you had a motive for killing him," continued Fisher, mildly. "You see, it's rather a curious situation. If you have a motive for murdering, you probably didn't murder. But if you hadn't any motive, why, then perhaps, you did."

"What on earth are you talking about?" demanded the duke, violently.

"It's quite simple," said Fisher. "When you went across he was either alive or dead. If he was alive, it might be you who killed him, or why should you have held your tongue about his death? But if he was dead, and you had a reason for killing him, you might have held your tongue for fear of being accused." Then after a silence he added, abstractedly: "Cyprus is a beautiful place, I believe. Romantic scenery and romantic people. Very intoxicating for a young man."

The duke suddenly clenched his hands and said, thickly, "Well, I had a motive."

"Then you're all right," said Fisher, holding out his hand with an air of huge relief. "I was pretty sure you wouldn't really do it; you had a fright when you saw it done, as was only natural. Like a bad dream come true, wasn't it?"

While this curious conversation was passing, Harker had gone into the house, disregarding the demonstrations of the sulky nephew, and came back presently with a new air of animation and a sheaf of papers in his hand.

"I've telephoned for the police," he said, stopping to speak to Fisher, "but I think I've done most of their work for them. I believe I've found out the truth. There's a paper here—" He stopped, for Fisher was looking at him with a singular expression; and it was Fisher who spoke next:

"Are there any papers that are not there, I wonder? I mean that are not there now?" After a pause he added: "Let us have the cards on the table. When you went through his papers in such a hurry, Harker, weren't you looking for something to—to make sure it shouldn't be found?"

Harker did not turn a red hair on his hard head, but he looked at the other out of the corners of his eyes.

"And I suppose," went on Fisher, smoothly, "that is why you, too, told us lies about having found Hook alive. You knew there was something to show that you might have killed him, and you didn't dare tell us he was killed. But, believe me, it's much better to be honest now."

Harker's haggard face suddenly lit up as if with infernal flames.

"Honest," he cried, "it's not so damned fine of you fellows to be honest. You're all born with silver spoons in your mouths, and then you swagger about with everlasting virtue because you haven't got other people's spoons in your pockets. But I was born in a Pimlico lodging house and I had to make my spoon, and there'd be plenty to say I only spoiled a horn or an honest man. And if a struggling man staggers a bit over the line in his youth, in the lower parts of the law which are pretty dingy, anyhow, there's always some old vampire to hang on to him all his life for it."

"Guatemalan Golcondas, wasn't it?" said Fisher, sympathetically.

Harker suddenly shuddered. Then he said, "I believe you must know everything, like God Almighty."

"I know too much," said Horne Fisher, "and all the wrong things."

The other three men were drawing nearer to them, but before they came too near, Harker said, in a voice that had recovered all its firmness:

"Yes, I did destroy a paper, but I really did find a paper, too; and

I believe that it clears us all."

"Very well," said Fisher, in a louder and more cheerful tone; "let us all have the benefit of it."

"On the very top of Sir Isaac's papers," explained Harker, "there was a threatening letter from a man named Hugo. It threatens to kill our unfortunate friend very much in the way that he was actually killed. It is a wild letter, full of taunts; you can see it for yourselves; but it makes a particular point of poor Hook's habit of fishing from the island. Above all, the man professes to be writing from a boat. And, since we alone went across to him," and he smiled in a rather ugly fashion, "the crime must have been committed by a man passing in a boat."

"Why, dear me!" cried the duke, with something almost amounting to animation. "Why, I remember the man called Hugo quite well! He was a sort of body servant and bodyguard of Sir Isaac. You see, Sir Isaac was in some fear of assault. He was—he was not very popular with several people. Hugo was discharged after some row or other; but I remember him well. He was a great big Hungarian fellow with great mustaches that stood out on each side of his face."

A door opened in the darkness of Harold March's memory, or, rather, oblivion, and showed a shining landscape, like that of a lost dream. It was rather a waterscape than a landscape, a thing of flooded meadows and low trees and the dark archway of a bridge. And for one instant he saw again the man with mustaches like dark horns leap up on to the bridge and disappear.

"Good heavens!" he cried. "Why, I met the murderer this morning!"

***

Horne Fisher and Harold March had their day on the river, after all, for the little group broke up when the police arrived. They declared that the coincidence of March's evidence had cleared the whole company, and clinched the case against the flying Hugo. Whether that Hungarian fugitive would ever be caught appeared to Horne Fisher to be highly doubtful; nor can it be pretended that he displayed any very demoniac detective energy in the matter as he leaned back in the boat cushions, smoking, and watching the swaying reeds slide past.

"It was a very good notion to hop up on to the bridge," he said. "An empty boat means very little; he hasn't been seen to land on either bank, and he's walked off the bridge without walking on to it, so to speak. He's got twenty-four hours' start; his mustaches will disappear, and then he will disappear. I think there is every hope of his escape."

"Hope?" repeated March, and stopped sculling for an instant.

"Yes, hope," repeated the other. "To begin with, I'm not going to be exactly consumed with Corsican revenge because somebody has killed Hook. Perhaps you may guess by this time what Hook was. A damned blood-sucking blackmailer was that simple, strenuous, self-made captain of industry. He had secrets against nearly everybody; one against poor old Westmoreland about an early marriage in Cyprus that might have put the duchess in a queer position; and one against Harker about some flutter with his client's money when he was a young solicitor. That's why they went to pieces when they found him murdered, of course. They felt as if they'd done it in a dream. But I admit I have another reason for not wanting our Hungarian friend actually hanged for the murder."

"And what is that?" asked his friend.

"Only that he didn't commit the murder," answered Fisher.

Harold March laid down the oars and let the boat drift for a moment.

"Do you know, I was half expecting something like that," he said. "It was quite irrational, but it was hanging about in the atmosphere, like thunder in the air."

"On the contrary, it's finding Hugo guilty that's irrational," replied Fisher. "Don't you see that they're condemning him for the very reason for which they acquit everybody else? Harker and Westmoreland were silent because they found him murdered, and knew there were papers that made them look like the murderers. Well, so did Hugo find him murdered, and so did Hugo know there was a paper that would make him look like the murderer. He had written it himself the day before."

"But in that case," said March, frowning, "at what sort of unearthly hour in the morning was the murder really committed? It was barely daylight when I met him at the bridge, and that's some way above the island."

"The answer is very simple," replied Fisher. "The crime was not committed in the morning. The crime was not committed on the island."

March stared at the shining water without replying, but Fisher resumed like one who had been asked a question:

"Every intelligent murder involves taking advantage of some one uncommon feature in a common situation. The feature here was the fancy of old Hook for being the first man up every morning, his fixed routine as an angler, and his annoyance at being disturbed. The murderer strangled him in his own house after dinner on the night before, carried his corpse, with all his fishing tackle, across the stream in the dead of night, tied him to the tree, and left him there under the stars. It was a dead man who sat fishing there all day. Then the murderer went back to the house, or, rather, to the garage, and went off in his motor car. The murderer drove his own motor car."

Fisher glanced at his friend's face and went on. "You look horrified, and the thing is horrible. But other things are horrible, too. If some obscure man had been hag-ridden by a blackmailer and had his family life ruined, you wouldn't think the murder of his persecutor the most inexcusable of murders. Is it any worse when a whole great nation is set free as well as a family? By this warning to Sweden we shall probably prevent war and not precipitate it, and save many thousand lives rather more valuable than the life of that viper. Oh, I'm not talking sophistry or seriously justifying the thing, but the slavery that held him and his country was a thousand times less justifiable. If I'd really been sharp I should have guessed it from his smooth, deadly smiling at dinner that night. Do you remember that silly talk about how old Isaac could always play his fish? In a pretty hellish sense he was a fisher of men."

Harold March took the oars and began to row again.

"I remember," he said, "and about how a big fish might break the line and get away."

VI. THE HOLE IN THE WALL

Two men, the one an architect and the other an archaeologist, met on the steps of the great house at Prior's Park; and their host, Lord Bulmer, in his breezy way, thought it natural to introduce them. It must be confessed that he was hazy as well as breezy, and had no very clear connection in his mind, beyond the sense that an architect and an archaeologist begin with the same series of letters. The world must remain in a reverent doubt as to whether he would, on the same principles, have presented a diplomatist to a dipsomaniac or a ratiocinator to a rat catcher. He was a big, fair, bull-necked young man, abounding in outward gestures, unconsciously flapping his gloves and flourishing his stick.

"You two ought to have something to talk about," he said, cheerfully. "Old buildings and all that sort of thing; this is rather an old building, by the way, though I say it who shouldn't. I must ask you to excuse me a moment; I've got to go and see about the cards for this Christmas romp my sister's arranging. We hope to see you all there, of course. Juliet wants it to be a fancy-dress affair—abbots and crusaders and all that. My ancestors, I suppose, after all."

"I trust the abbot was not an ancestor," said the archaeological gentleman, with a smile.

"Only a sort of great-uncle, I imagine," answered the other, laughing; then his rather rambling eye rolled round the ordered landscape in front of the house; an artificial sheet of water ornamented with an antiquated nymph in the center and surrounded by a park of tall trees now gray and black and frosty, for it was in the depth of a severe winter.

"It's getting jolly cold," his lordship continued. "My sister hopes we shall have some skating as well as dancing."

"If the crusaders come in full armor," said the other, "you must be careful not to drown your ancestors."

"Oh, there's no fear of that," answered Bulmer; "this precious lake of ours is not two feet deep anywhere." And with one of his flourishing gestures he stuck his stick into the water to demonstrate its shallowness. They could see the short end bent in the water, so that he seemed for a moment to lean his large weight on a breaking staff.

"The worst you can expect is to see an abbot sit down rather suddenly," he added, turning away. "Well, au revoir; I'll let you know about it later."

The archaeologist and the architect were left on the great stone steps smiling at each other; but whatever their common interests, they presented a considerable personal contrast, and the fanciful might even have found some contradiction in each considered individually. The former, a Mr. James Haddow, came from a drowsy den in the Inns of Court, full of leather and parchment, for the law was his profession and history only his hobby; he was indeed, among other things, the solicitor and agent of the Prior's Park estate. But he himself was far from drowsy and seemed remarkably wide awake, with shrewd and prominent blue eyes, and red hair brushed as neatly as his very neat costume. The latter, whose name was Leonard Crane, came straight from a crude and almost cockney office of builders and house agents in the neighboring suburb, sunning itself at the end of a new row of jerry-built houses with plans in very bright colors and notices in very large letters. But a serious observer, at a second glance, might have seen in his eyes something of that shining sleep that is called vision; and his yellow hair, while not affectedly long, was unaffectedly untidy. It was a manifest if melancholy truth that the architect was an artist. But the artistic temperament was far from explaining him; there was something else about him that was not definable, but which some even felt to be dangerous. Despite his dreaminess, he would sometimes surprise his friends with arts and even sports apart from his ordinary life, like memories of some previous existence. On this occasion, nevertheless, he hastened to disclaim any authority on the other man's hobby.

"I mustn't appear on false pretences," he said, with a smile. "I hardly even know what an archaeologist is, except that a rather rusty remnant of Greek suggests that he is a man who studies old things."

"Yes," replied Haddow, grimly. "An archaeologist is a man who studies old things and finds they are new."

Crane looked at him steadily for a moment and then smiled again.

"Dare one suggest," he said, "that some of the things we have been talking about are among the old things that turn out not to be old?"

His companion also was silent for a moment, and the smile on his rugged face was fainter as he replied, quietly:

"The wall round the park is really old. The one gate in it is Gothic, and I cannot find any trace of destruction or restoration. But the house and the estate generally—well the romantic ideas read into these things are often rather recent romances, things almost like fashionable novels. For instance, the very name of this place, Prior's Park, makes everybody think of it as a moonlit mediaeval abbey; I dare say the spiritualists by this time have discovered the ghost of a monk there. But, according to the only authoritative study of the matter I can find, the place was simply called Prior's as any rural place is called Podger's. It was the house of a Mr. Prior, a farmhouse, probably, that stood here at some time or other and was a local landmark. Oh, there are a great many examples of the same thing, here and everywhere else. This suburb of ours used to be a village, and because some of the people slurred the name and pronounced it Holliwell, many a minor poet indulged in fancies about a Holy Well, with spells and fairies and all the rest of it, filling the suburban drawing-rooms with the Celtic twilight. Whereas anyone acquainted with the facts knows that 'Hollinwall' simply means 'the hole in the wall,' and probably referred to some quite trivial accident. That's what I mean when I say that we don't so much find old things as we find new ones."

Crane seemed to have grown somewhat inattentive to the little lecture on antiquities and novelties, and the cause of his restlessness was soon apparent, and indeed approaching. Lord Bulmer's sister, Juliet Bray, was coming slowly across the lawn, accompanied by one gentleman and followed by two others. The young architect was in the illogical condition of mind in which he preferred three to one.

The man walking with the lady was no other than the eminent Prince Borodino, who was at least as famous as a distinguished diplomatist ought to be, in the interests of what is called secret diplomacy. He had been paying a round of visits at various English country houses, and exactly what he was doing for diplomacy at Prior's Park was as much a secret as any diplomatist could desire. The obvious thing to say of his appearance was that he would have been extremely handsome if he had not been entirely bald. But, indeed, that would itself be a rather bald way of putting it. Fantastic as it sounds, it would fit the case better to say that people would have been surprised to see hair growing on him; as surprised as if they had found hair growing on the bust of a Roman emperor. His tall figure was buttoned up in a tight-waisted fashion that rather accentuated his potential bulk, and he wore a red flower in his buttonhole. Of the two men walking behind one was also bald, but in a more partial and also a more premature fashion, for his drooping mustache was still yellow, and if his eyes were somewhat heavy it was with languor and not with age. It was Horne Fisher, and he was talking as easily and idly about everything as he always did. His companion was a more striking, and even more sinister, figure, and he had the added importance of being Lord Bulmer's oldest and most intimate friend. He was generally known with a severe simplicity as Mr. Brain; but it was understood that he had been a judge and police official in India, and that he had enemies, who had represented his measures against crime as themselves almost criminal. He was a brown skeleton of a man with dark, deep, sunken eyes and a black mustache that hid the meaning of his mouth. Though he had the look of one wasted by some tropical disease, his movements were much more alert than those of his lounging companion.

"It's all settled," announced the lady, with great animation, when they came within hailing distance. "You've all got to put on masquerade things and very likely skates as well, though the prince says they don't go with it; but we don't care about that. It's freezing already, and we don't often get such a chance in England."

"Even in India we don't exactly skate all the year round," observed

Mr. Brain.

"And even Italy is not primarily associated with ice," said the

Italian.

"Italy is primarily associated with ices," remarked Mr. Horne Fisher. "I mean with ice cream men. Most people in this country imagine that Italy is entirely populated with ice cream men and organ grinders. There certainly are a lot of them; perhaps they're an invading army in disguise."

"How do you know they are not the secret emissaries of our diplomacy?" asked the prince, with a slightly scornful smile. "An army of organ grinders might pick up hints, and their monkeys might pick up all sort of things."

"The organs are organized in fact," said the flippant Mr. Fisher.

"Well, I've known it pretty cold before now in Italy and even in

India, up on the Himalayan slopes. The ice on our own little round

pond will be quite cozy by comparison."

Juliet Bray was an attractive lady with dark hair and eyebrows and dancing eyes, and there was a geniality and even generosity in her rather imperious ways. In most matters she could command her brother, though that nobleman, like many other men of vague ideas, was not without a touch of the bully when he was at bay. She could certainly command her guests, even to the extent of decking out the most respectable and reluctant of them with her mediaeval masquerade. And it really seemed as if she could command the elements also, like a witch. For the weather steadily hardened and sharpened; that night the ice of the lake, glimmering in the moonlight, was like a marble floor, and they had begun to dance and skate on it before it was dark.

Prior's Park, or, more properly, the surrounding district of Holinwall, was a country seat that had become a suburb; having once had only a dependent village at its doors, it now found outside all its doors the signals of the expansion of London. Mr. Haddow, who was engaged in historical researches both in the library and the locality, could find little assistance in the latter. He had already realized, from the documents, that Prior's Park had originally been something like Prior's Farm, named after some local figure, but the new social conditions were all against his tracing the story by its traditions. Had any of the real rustics remained, he would probably have found some lingering legend of Mr. Prior, however remote he might be. But the new nomadic population of clerks and artisans, constantly shifting their homes from one suburb to another, or their children from one school to another, could have no corporate continuity. They had all that forgetfulness of history that goes everywhere with the extension of education.

Nevertheless, when he came out of the library next morning and saw the wintry trees standing round the frozen pond like a black forest, he felt he might well have been far in the depths of the country. The old wall running round the park kept that inclosure itself still entirely rural and romantic, and one could easily imagine that the depths of that dark forest faded away indefinitely into distant vales and hills. The gray and black and silver of the wintry wood were all the more severe or somber as a contrast to the colored carnival groups that already stood on and around the frozen pool. For the house party had already flung themselves impatiently into fancy dress, and the lawyer, with his neat black suit and red hair, was the only modern figure among them.

"Aren't you going to dress up?" asked Juliet, indignantly shaking at him a horned and towering blue headdress of the fourteenth century which framed her face very becomingly, fantastic as it was. "Everybody here has to be in the Middle Ages. Even Mr. Brain has put on a sort of brown dressing gown and says he's a monk; and Mr. Fisher got hold of some old potato sacks in the kitchen and sewed them together; he's supposed to be a monk, too. As to the prince, he's perfectly glorious, in great crimson robes as a cardinal. He looks as if he could poison everybody. You simply must be something."

"I will be something later in the day," he replied. "At present I am nothing but an antiquary and an attorney. I have to see your brother presently, about some legal business and also some local investigations he asked me to make. I must look a little like a steward when I give an account of my stewardship."

"Oh, but my brother has dressed up!" cried the girl. "Very much so. No end, if I may say so. Why he's bearing down on you now in all his glory."

The noble lord was indeed marching toward them in a magnificent sixteenth-century costume of purple and gold, with a gold-hilted sword and a plumed cap, and manners to match. Indeed, there was something more than his usual expansiveness of bodily action in his appearance at that moment. It almost seemed, so to speak, that the plumes on his hat had gone to his head. He flapped his great, gold-lined cloak like the wings of a fairy king in a pantomime; he even drew his sword with a flourish and waved it about as he did his walking stick. In the light of after events there seemed to be something monstrous and ominous about that exuberance, something of the spirit that is called fey. At the time it merely crossed a few people's minds that he might possibly be drunk.

As he strode toward his sister the first figure he passed was that of Leonard Crane, clad in Lincoln green, with the horn and baldrick and sword appropriate to Robin Hood; for he was standing nearest to the lady, where, indeed, he might have been found during a disproportionate part of the time. He had displayed one of his buried talents in the matter of skating, and now that the skating was over seemed disposed to prolong the partnership. The boisterous Bulmer playfully made a pass at him with his drawn sword, going forward with the lunge in the proper fencing fashion, and making a somewhat too familiar Shakespearean quotation about a rodent and a Venetian coin.

Probably in Crane also there was a subdued excitement just then; anyhow, in one flash he had drawn his own sword and parried; and then suddenly, to the surprise of everyone, Bulmer's weapon seemed to spring out of his hand into the air and rolled away on the ringing ice.

"Well, I never!" said the lady, as if with justifiable indignation.

"You never told me you could fence, too."

Bulmer put up his sword with an air rather bewildered than annoyed, which increased the impression of something irresponsible in his mood at the moment; then he turned rather abruptly to his lawyer, saying:

"We can settle up about the estate after dinner; I've missed nearly all the skating as it is, and I doubt if the ice will hold till to-morrow night. I think I shall get up early and have a spin by myself."

"You won't be disturbed with my company," said Horne Fisher, in his weary fashion. "If I have to begin the day with ice, in the American fashion, I prefer it in smaller quantities. But no early hours for me in December. The early bird catches the cold."

"Oh, I shan't die of catching a cold," answered Bulmer, and laughed.

***

A considerable group of the skating party had consisted of the guests staying at the house, and the rest had tailed off in twos and threes some time before most of the guests began to retire for the night. Neighbors, always invited to Prior's Park on such occasions, went back to their own houses in motors or on foot; the legal and archeological gentleman had returned to the Inns of Court by a late train, to get a paper called for during his consultation with his client; and most of the other guests were drifting and lingering at various stages on their way up to bed. Horne Fisher, as if to deprive himself of any excuse for his refusal of early rising, had been the first to retire to his room; but, sleepy as he looked, he could not sleep. He had picked up from a table the book of antiquarian topography, in which Haddow had found his first hints about the origin of the local name, and, being a man with a quiet and quaint capacity for being interested in anything, he began to read it steadily, making notes now and then of details on which his previous reading left him with a certain doubt about his present conclusions. His room was the one nearest to the lake in the center of the woods, and was therefore the quietest, and none of the last echoes of the evening's festivity could reach him. He had followed carefully the argument which established the derivation from Mr. Prior's farm and the hole in the wall, and disposed of any fashionable fancy about monks and magic wells, when he began to be conscious of a noise audible in the frozen silence of the night. It was not a particularly loud noise, but it seemed to consist of a series of thuds or heavy blows, such as might be struck on a wooden door by a man seeking to enter. They were followed by something like a faint creak or crack, as if the obstacle had either been opened or had given way. He opened his own bedroom door and listened, but as he heard talk and laughter all over the lower floors, he had no reason to fear that a summons would be neglected or the house left without protection. He went to his open window, looking out over the frozen pond and the moonlit statue in the middle of their circle of darkling woods, and listened again. But silence had returned to that silent place, and, after straining his ears for a considerable time, he could hear nothing but the solitary hoot of a distant departing train. Then he reminded himself how many nameless noises can be heard by the wakeful during the most ordinary night, and shrugging his shoulders, went wearily to bed.

He awoke suddenly and sat up in bed with his ears filled, as with thunder, with the throbbing echoes of a rending cry. He remained rigid for a moment, and then sprang out of bed, throwing on the loose gown of sacking he had worn all day. He went first to the window, which was open, but covered with a thick curtain, so that his room was still completely dark; but when he tossed the curtain aside and put his head out, he saw that a gray and silver daybreak had already appeared behind the black woods that surrounded the little lake, and that was all that he did see. Though the sound had certainly come in through the open window from this direction, the whole scene was still and empty under the morning light as under the moonlight. Then the long, rather lackadaisical hand he had laid on a window sill gripped it tighter, as if to master a tremor, and his peering blue eyes grew bleak with fear. It may seem that his emotion was exaggerated and needless, considering the effort of common sense by which he had conquered his nervousness about the noise on the previous night. But that had been a very different sort of noise. It might have been made by half a hundred things, from the chopping of wood to the breaking of bottles. There was only one thing in nature from which could come the sound that echoed through the dark house at daybreak. It was the awful articulate voice of man; and it was something worse, for he knew what man.

He knew also that it had been a shout for help. It seemed to him that he had heard the very word; but the word, short as it was, had been swallowed up, as if the man had been stifled or snatched away even as he spoke. Only the mocking reverberations of it remained even in his memory, but he had no doubt of the original voice. He had no doubt that the great bull's voice of Francis Bray, Baron Bulmer, had been heard for the last time between the darkness and the lifting dawn.

How long he stood there he never knew, but he was startled into life by the first living thing that he saw stirring in that half-frozen landscape. Along the path beside the lake, and immediately under his window, a figure was walking slowly and softly, but with great composure—a stately figure in robes of a splendid scarlet; it was the Italian prince, still in his cardinal's costume. Most of the company had indeed lived in their costumes for the last day or two, and Fisher himself had assumed his frock of sacking as a convenient dressing gown; but there seemed, nevertheless, something unusually finished and formal, in the way of an early bird, about this magnificent red cockatoo. It was as if the early bird had been up all night.

"What is the matter?" he called, sharply, leaning out of the window, and the Italian turned up his great yellow face like a mask of brass.

"We had better discuss it downstairs," said Prince Borodino.

Fisher ran downstairs, and encountered the great, red-robed figure entering the doorway and blocking the entrance with his bulk.

"Did you hear that cry?" demanded Fisher.

"I heard a noise and I came out," answered the diplomatist, and his face was too dark in the shadow for its expression to be read.

"It was Bulmer's voice," insisted Fisher. "I'll swear it was

Bulmer's voice."

"Did you know him well?" asked the other.

The question seemed irrelevant, though it was not illogical, and Fisher could only answer in a random fashion that he knew Lord Bulmer only slightly.

"Nobody seems to have known him well," continued the Italian, in level tones. "Nobody except that man Brain. Brain is rather older than Bulmer, but I fancy they shared a good many secrets."

Fisher moved abruptly, as if waking from a momentary trance, and said, in a new and more vigorous voice, "But look here, hadn't we better get outside and see if anything has happened."

"The ice seems to be thawing," said the other, almost with indifference.

When they emerged from the house, dark stains and stars in the gray field of ice did indeed indicate that the frost was breaking up, as their host had prophesied the day before, and the very memory of yesterday brought back the mystery of to-day.

"He knew there would be a thaw," observed the prince. "He went out skating quite early on purpose. Did he call out because he landed in the water, do you think?"

Fisher looked puzzled. "Bulmer was the last man to bellow like that because he got his boots wet. And that's all he could do here; the water would hardly come up to the calf of a man of his size. You can see the flat weeds on the floor of the lake, as if it were through a thin pane of glass. No, if Bulmer had only broken the ice he wouldn't have said much at the moment, though possibly a good deal afterward. We should have found him stamping and damning up and down this path, and calling for clean boots."

"Let us hope we shall find him as happily employed," remarked the diplomatist. "In that case the voice must have come out of the wood."

"I'll swear it didn't come out of the house," said Fisher; and the two disappeared together into the twilight of wintry trees.

The plantation stood dark against the fiery colors of sunrise, a black fringe having that feathery appearance which makes trees when they are bare the very reverse of rugged. Hours and hours afterward, when the same dense, but delicate, margin was dark against the greenish colors opposite the sunset, the search thus begun at sunrise had not come to an end. By successive stages, and to slowly gathering groups of the company, it became apparent that the most extraordinary of all gaps had appeared in the party; the guests could find no trace of their host anywhere. The servants reported that his bed had been slept in and his skates and his fancy costume were gone, as if he had risen early for the purpose he had himself avowed. But from the top of the house to the bottom, from the walls round the park to the pond in the center, there was no trace of Lord Bulmer, dead or alive. Horne Fisher realized that a chilling premonition had already prevented him from expecting to find the man alive. But his bald brow was wrinkled over an entirely new and unnatural problem, in not finding the man at all.

He considered the possibility of Bulmer having gone off of his own accord, for some reason; but after fully weighing it he finally dismissed it. It was inconsistent with the unmistakable voice heard at daybreak, and with many other practical obstacles. There was only one gateway in the ancient and lofty wall round the small park; the lodge keeper kept it locked till late in the morning, and the lodge keeper had seen no one pass. Fisher was fairly sure that he had before him a mathematical problem in an inclosed space. His instinct had been from the first so attuned to the tragedy that it would have been almost a relief to him to find the corpse. He would have been grieved, but not horrified, to come on the nobleman's body dangling from one of his own trees as from a gibbet, or floating in his own pool like a pallid weed. What horrified him was to find nothing.

He soon become conscious that he was not alone even in his most individual and isolated experiments. He often found a figure following him like his shadow, in silent and almost secret clearings in the plantation or outlying nooks and corners of the old wall. The dark-mustached mouth was as mute as the deep eyes were mobile, darting incessantly hither and thither, but it was clear that Brain of the Indian police had taken up the trail like an old hunter after a tiger. Seeing that he was the only personal friend of the vanished man, this seemed natural enough, and Fisher resolved to deal frankly with him.

"This silence is rather a social strain," he said. "May I break the ice by talking about the weather?—which, by the way, has already broken the ice. I know that breaking the ice might be a rather melancholy metaphor in this case."

"I don't think so," replied Brain, shortly. "I don't fancy the ice had much to do with it. I don't see how it could."

"What would you propose doing?" asked Fisher.

"Well, we've sent for the authorities, of course, but I hope to find something out before they come," replied the Anglo-Indian. "I can't say I have much hope from police methods in this country. Too much red tape, habeas corpus and that sort of thing. What we want is to see that nobody bolts; the nearest we could get to it would be to collect the company and count them, so to speak. Nobody's left lately, except that lawyer who was poking about for antiquities."

"Oh, he's out of it; he left last night," answered the other. "Eight hours after Bulmer's chauffeur saw his lawyer off by the train I heard Bulmer's own voice as plain as I hear yours now."

"I suppose you don't believe in spirits?" said the man from India. After a pause he added: "There's somebody else I should like to find, before we go after a fellow with an alibi in the Inner Temple. What's become of that fellow in green—the architect dressed up as a forester? I haven't seem him about."

Mr. Brain managed to secure his assembly of all the distracted company before the arrival of the police. But when he first began to comment once more on the young architect's delay in putting in an appearance, he found himself in the presence of a minor mystery, and a psychological development of an entirely unexpected kind.

Juliet Bray had confronted the catastrophe of her brother's disappearance with a somber stoicism in which there was, perhaps, more paralysis than pain; but when the other question came to the surface she was both agitated and angry.

"We don't want to jump to any conclusions about anybody," Brain was saying in his staccato style. "But we should like to know a little more about Mr. Crane. Nobody seems to know much about him, or where he comes from. And it seems a sort of coincidence that yesterday he actually crossed swords with poor Bulmer, and could have stuck him, too, since he showed himself the better swordsman. Of course, that may be an accident and couldn't possibly be called a case against anybody; but then we haven't the means to make a real case against anybody. Till the police come we are only a pack of very amateur sleuthhounds."

"And I think you're a pack of snobs," said Juliet. "Because Mr. Crane is a genius who's made his own way, you try to suggest he's a murderer without daring to say so. Because he wore a toy sword and happened to know how to use it, you want us to believe he used it like a bloodthirsty maniac for no reason in the world. And because he could have hit my brother and didn't, you deduce that he did. That's the sort of way you argue. And as for his having disappeared, you're wrong in that as you are in everything else, for here he comes."

And, indeed, the green figure of the fictitious Robin Hood slowly detached itself from the gray background of the trees, and came toward them as she spoke.

He approached the group slowly, but with composure; but he was decidedly pale, and the eyes of Brain and Fisher had already taken in one detail of the green-clad figure more clearly than all the rest. The horn still swung from his baldrick, but the sword was gone.

Rather to the surprise of the company, Brain did not follow up the question thus suggested; but, while retaining an air of leading the inquiry, had also an appearance of changing the subject.

"Now we're all assembled," he observed, quietly, "there is a question I want to ask to begin with. Did anybody here actually see Lord Bulmer this morning?"

Leonard Crane turned his pale face round the circle of faces till he came to Juliet's; then he compressed his lips a little and said:

"Yes, I saw him."

"Was he alive and well?" asked Brain, quickly. "How was he dressed?"

"He appeared exceedingly well," replied Crane, with a curious intonation. "He was dressed as he was yesterday, in that purple costume copied from the portrait of his ancestor in the sixteenth century. He had his skates in his hand."

"And his sword at his side, I suppose," added the questioner. "Where is your own sword, Mr. Crane?"

"I threw it away."

In the singular silence that ensued, the train of thought in many minds became involuntarily a series of colored pictures.

They had grown used to their fanciful garments looking more gay and gorgeous against the dark gray and streaky silver of the forest, so that the moving figures glowed like stained-glass saints walking. The effect had been more fitting because so many of them had idly parodied pontifical or monastic dress. But the most arresting attitude that remained in their memories had been anything but merely monastic; that of the moment when the figure in bright green and the other in vivid violet had for a moment made a silver cross of their crossing swords. Even when it was a jest it had been something of a drama; and it was a strange and sinister thought that in the gray daybreak the same figures in the same posture might have been repeated as a tragedy.

"Did you quarrel with him?" asked Brain, suddenly.

"Yes," replied the immovable man in green. "Or he quarreled with me."

"Why did he quarrel with you?" asked the investigator; and Leonard

Crane made no reply.

Horne Fisher, curiously enough, had only given half his attention to this crucial cross-examination. His heavy-lidded eyes had languidly followed the figure of Prince Borodino, who at this stage had strolled away toward the fringe of the wood; and, after a pause, as of meditation, had disappeared into the darkness of the trees.

He was recalled from his irrelevance by the voice of Juliet Bray, which rang out with an altogether new note of decision:

"If that is the difficulty, it had best be cleared up. I am engaged to Mr. Crane, and when we told my brother he did not approve of it; that is all."

Neither Brain nor Fisher exhibited any surprise, but the former added, quietly:

"Except, I suppose, that he and your brother went off into the wood to discuss it, where Mr. Crane mislaid his sword, not to mention his companion."

"And may I ask," inquired Crane, with a certain flicker of mockery passing over his pallid features, "what I am supposed to have done with either of them? Let us adopt the cheerful thesis that I am a murderer; it has yet to be shown that I am a magician. If I ran your unfortunate friend through the body, what did I do with the body? Did I have it carried away by seven flying dragons, or was it merely a trifling matter of turning it into a milk-white hind?"

"It is no occasion for sneering," said the Anglo-Indian judge, with abrupt authority. "It doesn't make it look better for you that you can joke about the loss."

Fisher's dreamy, and even dreary, eye was still on the edge of the wood behind, and he became conscious of masses of dark red, like a stormy sunset cloud, glowing through the gray network of the thin trees, and the prince in his cardinal's robes reemerged on to the pathway. Brain had had half a notion that the prince might have gone to look for the lost rapier. But when he reappeared he was carrying in his hand, not a sword, but an ax.

The incongruity between the masquerade and the mystery had created a curious psychological atmosphere. At first they had all felt horribly ashamed at being caught in the foolish disguises of a festival, by an event that had only too much the character of a funeral. Many of them would have already gone back and dressed in clothes that were more funereal or at least more formal. But somehow at the moment this seemed like a second masquerade, more artificial and frivolous than the first. And as they reconciled themselves to their ridiculous trappings, a curious sensation had come over some of them, notably over the more sensitive, like Crane and Fisher and Juliet, but in some degree over everybody except the practical Mr. Brain. It was almost as if they were the ghosts of their own ancestors haunting that dark wood and dismal lake, and playing some old part that they only half remembered. The movements of those colored figures seemed to mean something that had been settled long before, like a silent heraldry. Acts, attitudes, external objects, were accepted as an allegory even without the key; and they knew when a crisis had come, when they did not know what it was. And somehow they knew subconsciously that the whole tale had taken a new and terrible turn, when they saw the prince stand in the gap of the gaunt trees, in his robes of angry crimson and with his lowering face of bronze, bearing in his hand a new shape of death. They could not have named a reason, but the two swords seemed indeed to have become toy swords and the whole tale of them broken and tossed away like a toy. Borodino looked like the Old World headsman, clad in terrible red, and carrying the ax for the execution of the criminal. And the criminal was not Crane.

Mr. Brain of the Indian police was glaring at the new object, and it was a moment or two before he spoke, harshly and almost hoarsely.

"What are you doing with that?" he asked. "Seems to be a woodman's chopper."

"A natural association of ideas," observed Horne Fisher. "If you meet a cat in a wood you think it's a wildcat, though it may have just strolled from the drawing-room sofa. As a matter of fact, I happen to know that is not the woodman's chopper. It's the kitchen chopper, or meat ax, or something like that, that somebody has thrown away in the wood. I saw it in the kitchen myself when I was getting the potato sacks with which I reconstructed a mediaeval hermit."

"All the same, it is not without interest," remarked the prince, holding out the instrument to Fisher, who took it and examined it carefully. "A butcher's cleaver that has done butcher's work."

"It was certainly the instrument of the crime," assented Fisher, in a low voice.

Brain was staring at the dull blue gleam of the ax head with fierce and fascinated eyes. "I don't understand you," he said. "There is no—there are no marks on it."

"It has shed no blood," answered Fisher, "but for all that it has committed a crime. This is as near as the criminal came to the crime when he committed it."

"What do you mean?"

"He was not there when he did it," explained Fisher. "It's a poor sort of murderer who can't murder people when he isn't there."

"You seem to be talking merely for the sake of mystification," said Brain. "If you have any practical advice to give you might as well make it intelligible."

"The only practical advice I can suggest," said Fisher, thoughtfully, "is a little research into local topography and nomenclature. They say there used to be a Mr. Prior, who had a farm in this neighborhood. I think some details about the domestic life of the late Mr. Prior would throw a light on this terrible business."

"And you have nothing more immediate than your topography to offer," said Brain, with a sneer, "to help me avenge my friend?"

"Well," said Fisher, "I should find out the truth about the Hole in the Wall."

***

That night, at the close of a stormy twilight and under a strong west wind that followed the breaking of the frost, Leonard Crane was wending his way in a wild rotatory walk round and round the high, continuous wall that inclosed the little wood. He was driven by a desperate idea of solving for himself the riddle that had clouded his reputation and already even threatened his liberty. The police authorities, now in charge of the inquiry, had not arrested him, but he knew well enough that if he tried to move far afield he would be instantly arrested. Horne Fisher's fragmentary hints, though he had refused to expand them as yet, had stirred the artistic temperament of the architect to a sort of wild analysis, and he was resolved to read the hieroglyph upside down and every way until it made sense. If it was something connected with a hole in the wall he would find the hole in the wall; but, as a matter of fact, he was unable to find the faintest crack in the wall. His professional knowledge told him that the masonry was all of one workmanship and one date, and, except for the regular entrance, which threw no light on the mystery, he found nothing suggesting any sort of hiding place or means of escape. Walking a narrow path between the winding wall and the wild eastward bend and sweep of the gray and feathery trees, seeing shifting gleams of a lost sunset winking almost like lightning as the clouds of tempest scudded across the sky and mingling with the first faint blue light from a slowly strengthened moon behind him, he began to feel his head going round as his heels were going round and round the blind recurrent barrier. He had thoughts on the border of thought; fancies about a fourth dimension which was itself a hole to hide anything, of seeing everything from a new angle out of a new window in the senses; or of some mystical light and transparency, like the new rays of chemistry, in which he could see Bulmer's body, horrible and glaring, floating in a lurid halo over the woods and the wall. He was haunted also with the hint, which somehow seemed to be equally horrifying, that it all had something to do with Mr. Prior. There seemed even to be something creepy in the fact that he was always respectfully referred to as Mr. Prior, and that it was in the domestic life of the dead farmer that he had been bidden to seek the seed of these dreadful things. As a matter of fact, he had found that no local inquiries had revealed anything at all about the Prior family.

The moonlight had broadened and brightened, the wind had driven off the clouds and itself died fitfully away, when he came round again to the artificial lake in front of the house. For some reason it looked a very artificial lake; indeed, the whole scene was like a classical landscape with a touch of Watteau; the Palladian facade of the house pale in the moon, and the same silver touching the very pagan and naked marble nymph in the middle of the pond. Rather to his surprise, he found another figure there beside the statue, sitting almost equally motionless; and the same silver pencil traced the wrinkled brow and patient face of Horne Fisher, still dressed as a hermit and apparently practicing something of the solitude of a hermit. Nevertheless, he looked up at Leonard Crane and smiled, almost as if he had expected him.

"Look here," said Crane, planting himself in front of him, "can you tell me anything about this business?"

"I shall soon have to tell everybody everything about it," replied Fisher, "but I've no objection to telling you something first. But, to begin with, will you tell me something? What really happened when you met Bulmer this morning? You did throw away your sword, but you didn't kill him."

"I didn't kill him because I threw away my sword," said the other.

"I did it on purpose—or I'm not sure what might have happened."

After a pause he went on, quietly: "The late Lord Bulmer was a very breezy gentleman, extremely breezy. He was very genial with his inferiors, and would have his lawyer and his architect staying in his house for all sorts of holidays and amusements. But there was another side to him, which they found out when they tried to be his equals. When I told him that his sister and I were engaged, something happened which I simply can't and won't describe. It seemed to me like some monstrous upheaval of madness. But I suppose the truth is painfully simple. There is such a thing as the coarseness of a gentleman. And it is the most horrible thing in humanity."

"I know," said Fisher. "The Renaissance nobles of the Tudor time were like that."

"It is odd that you should say that," Crane went on. "For while we were talking there came on me a curious feeling that we were repeating some scene of the past, and that I was really some outlaw, found in the woods like Robin

Hood, and that he had really stepped in all his plumes and purple out of the picture frame of the ancestral portrait. Anyhow, he was the man in possession, and he neither feared God nor regarded man. I defied him, of course, and walked away. I might really have killed him if I had not walked away."

"Yes," said Fisher, nodding, "his ancestor was in possession and he was in possession, and this is the end of the story. It all fits in."

"Fits in with what?" cried his companion, with sudden impatience. "I can't make head or tail of it. You tell me to look for the secret in the hole in the wall, but I can't find any hole in the wall."

"There isn't any," said Fisher. "That's the secret." After reflecting a moment, he added: "Unless you call it a hole in the wall of the world. Look here; I'll tell you if you like, but I'm afraid it involves an introduction. You've got to understand one of the tricks of the modern mind, a tendency that most people obey without noticing it. In the village or suburb outside there's an inn with the sign of St. George and the Dragon. Now suppose I went about telling everybody that this was only a corruption of King George and the Dragoon. Scores of people would believe it, without any inquiry, from a vague feeling that it's probable because it's prosaic. It turns something romantic and legendary into something recent and ordinary. And that somehow makes it sound rational, though it is unsupported by reason. Of course some people would have the sense to remember having seen St. George in old Italian pictures and French romances, but a good many wouldn't think about it at all. They would just swallow the skepticism because it was skepticism. Modern intelligence won't accept anything on authority. But it will accept anything without authority. That's exactly what has happened here.

"When some critic or other chose to say that Prior's Park was not a priory, but was named after some quite modern man named Prior, nobody really tested the theory at all. It never occurred to anybody repeating the story to ask if there was any Mr. Prior, if anybody had ever seen him or heard of him. As a matter of fact, it was a priory, and shared the fate of most priories—that is, the Tudor gentleman with the plumes simply stole it by brute force and turned it into his own private house; he did worse things, as you shall hear. But the point here is that this is how the trick works, and the trick works in the same way in the other part of the tale. The name of this district is printed Holinwall in all the best maps produced by the scholars; and they allude lightly, not without a smile, to the fact that it was pronounced Holiwell by the most ignorant and old-fashioned of the poor. But it is spelled wrong and pronounced right."

"Do you mean to say," asked Crane, quickly, "that there really was a well?"

"There is a well," said Fisher, "and the truth lies at the bottom of it."

As he spoke he stretched out his hand and pointed toward the sheet of water in front of him.

"The well is under that water somewhere," he said, "and this is not the first tragedy connected with it. The founder of this house did something which his fellow ruffians very seldom did; something that had to be hushed up even in the anarchy of the pillage of the monasteries. The well was connected with the miracles of some saint, and the last prior that guarded it was something like a saint himself; certainly he was something very like a martyr. He defied the new owner and dared him to pollute the place, till the noble, in a fury, stabbed him and flung his body into the well, whither, after four hundred years, it has been followed by an heir of the usurper, clad in the same purple and walking the world with the same pride."

"But how did it happen," demanded Crane, "that for the first time

Bulmer fell in at that particular spot?"

"Because the ice was only loosened at that particular spot, by the only man who knew it," answered Horne Fisher. "It was cracked deliberately, with the kitchen chopper, at that special place; and I myself heard the hammering and did not understand it. The place had been covered with an artificial lake, if only because the whole truth had to be covered with an artificial legend. But don't you see that it is exactly what those pagan nobles would have done, to desecrate it with a sort of heathen goddess, as the Roman Emperor built a temple to Venus on the Holy Sepulchre. But the truth could still be traced out, by any scholarly man determined to trace it. And this man was determined to trace it."

"What man?" asked the other, with a shadow of the answer in his mind.

"The only man who has an alibi," replied Fisher. "James Haddow, the antiquarian lawyer, left the night before the fatality, but he left that black star of death on the ice. He left abruptly, having previously proposed to stay; probably, I think, after an ugly scene with Bulmer, at their legal interview. As you know yourself, Bulmer could make a man feel pretty murderous, and I rather fancy the lawyer had himself irregularities to confess, and was in danger of exposure by his client. But it's my reading of human nature that a man will cheat in his trade, but not in his hobby. Haddow may have been a dishonest lawyer, but he couldn't help being an honest antiquary. When he got on the track of the truth about the Holy Well he had to follow it up; he was not to be bamboozled with newspaper anecdotes about Mr. Prior and a hole in the wall; he found out everything, even to the exact location of the well, and he was rewarded, if being a successful assassin can be regarded as a reward."

"And how did you get on the track of all this hidden history?" asked the young architect.

A cloud came across the brow of Horne Fisher. "I knew only too much about it already," he said, "and, after all, it's shameful for me to be speaking lightly of poor Bulmer, who has paid his penalty; but the rest of us haven't. I dare say every cigar I smoke and every liqueur I drink comes directly or indirectly from the harrying of the holy places and the persecution of the poor. After all, it needs very little poking about in the past to find that hole in the wall, that great breach in the defenses of English history. It lies just under the surface of a thin sheet of sham information and instruction, just as the black and blood-stained well lies just under that floor of shallow water and flat weeds. Oh, the ice is thin, but it bears; it is strong enough to support us when we dress up as monks and dance on it, in mockery of the dear, quaint old Middle Ages. They told me I must put on fancy dress; so I did put on fancy dress, according to my own taste and fancy. I put on the only costume I think fit for a man who has inherited the position of a gentleman, and yet has not entirely lost the feelings of one."

In answer to a look of inquiry, he rose with a sweeping and downward gesture.

"Sackcloth," he said; "and I would wear the ashes as well if they would stay on my bald head."

VII. THE TEMPLE OF SILENCE

Harold March and the few who cultivated the friendship of Horne Fisher, especially if they saw something of him in his own social setting, were conscious of a certain solitude in his very sociability. They seemed to be always meeting his relations and never meeting his family. Perhaps it would be truer to say that they saw much of his family and nothing of his home. His cousins and connections ramified like a labyrinth all over the governing class of Great Britain, and he seemed to be on good, or at least on good-humored, terms with most of them. For Horne Fisher was remarkable for a curious impersonal information and interest touching all sorts of topics, so that one could sometimes fancy that his culture, like his colorless, fair mustache and pale, drooping features, had the neutral nature of a chameleon. Anyhow, he could always get on with viceroys and Cabinet Ministers and all the great men responsible for great departments, and talk to each of them on his own subject, on the branch of study with which he was most seriously concerned. Thus he could converse with the Minister for War about silkworms, with the Minister of Education about detective stories, with the Minister of Labor about

Limoges enamel, and with the Minister of Missions and Moral Progress (if that be his correct title) about the pantomime boys of the last four decades. And as the first was his first cousin, the second his second cousin, the third his brother-in-law, and the fourth his uncle by marriage, this conversational versatility certainly served in one sense to create a happy family. But March never seemed to get a glimpse of that domestic interior to which men of the middle classes are accustomed in their friendships, and which is indeed the foundation of friendship and love and everything else in any sane and stable society. He wondered whether Horne Fisher was both an orphan and an only child.

It was, therefore, with something like a start that he found that Fisher had a brother, much more prosperous and powerful than himself, though hardly, March thought, so entertaining. Sir Henry Harland Fisher, with half the alphabet after his name, was something at the Foreign Office far more tremendous than the Foreign Secretary. Apparently, it ran in the family, after all; for it seemed there was another brother, Ashton Fisher, in India, rather more tremendous than the Viceroy. Sir Henry Fisher was a heavier, but handsomer edition of his brother, with a brow equally bald, but much more smooth. He was very courteous, but a shade patronizing, not only to March, but even, as March fancied, to Horne Fisher as well. The latter gentleman, who had many intuitions about the half-formed thoughts of others, glanced at the topic himself as they came away from the great house in Berkeley Square.

"Why, don't you know," he observed quietly, "that I am the fool of the family?"

"It must be a clever family," said Harold March, with a smile.

"Very gracefully expressed," replied Fisher; "that is the best of having a literary training. Well, perhaps it is an exaggeration to say I am the fool of the family. It's enough to say I am the failure of the family."

"It seems queer to me that you should fail especially," remarked the journalist. "As they say in the examinations, what did you fail in?"

"Politics," replied his friend. "I stood for Parliament when I was quite a young man and got in by an enormous majority, with loud cheers and chairing round the town. Since then, of course, I've been rather under a cloud."

"I'm afraid I don't quite understand the 'of course,'" answered

March, laughing.

"That part of it isn't worth understanding," said Fisher. "But as a matter of fact, old chap, the other part of it was rather odd and interesting. Quite a detective story in its way, as well as the first lesson I had in what modern politics are made of. If you like, I'll tell you all about it." And the following, recast in a less allusive and conversational manner, is the story that he told.

Nobody privileged of late years to meet Sir Henry Harland Fisher would believe that he had ever been called Harry. But, indeed, he had been boyish enough when a boy, and that serenity which shone on him through life, and which now took the form of gravity, had once taken the form of gayety. His friends would have said that he was all the more ripe in his maturity for having been young in his youth. His enemies would have said that he was still light minded, but no longer light hearted. But in any case, the whole of the story Horne Fisher had to tell arose out of the accident which had made young Harry Fisher private secretary to Lord Saltoun. Hence his later connection with the Foreign Office, which had, indeed, come to him as a sort of legacy from his lordship when that great man was the power behind the throne. This is not the place to say much about Saltoun, little as was known of him and much as there was worth knowing. England has had at least three or four such secret statesmen. An aristocratic polity produces every now and then an aristocrat who is also an accident, a man of intellectual independence and insight, a Napoleon born in the purple. His vast work was mostly invisible, and very little could be got out of him in private life except a crusty and rather cynical sense of humor. But it was certainly the accident of his presence at a family dinner of the Fishers, and the unexpected opinion he expressed, which turned what might have been a dinner-table joke into a sort of small sensational novel.

Save for Lord Saltoun, it was a family party of Fishers, for the only other distinguished stranger had just departed after dinner, leaving the rest to their coffee and cigars. This had been a figure of some interest—a young Cambridge man named Eric Hughes who was the rising hope of the party of Reform, to which the Fisher family, along with their friend Saltoun, had long been at least formally attached. The personality of Hughes was substantially summed up in the fact that he talked eloquently and earnestly through the whole dinner, but left immediately after to be in time for an appointment. All his actions had something at once ambitious and conscientious; he drank no wine, but was slightly intoxicated with words. And his face and phrases were on the front page of all the newspapers just then, because he was contesting the safe seat of Sir Francis Verner in the great by-election in the west. Everybody was talking about the powerful speech against squirarchy which he had just delivered; even in the Fisher circle everybody talked about it except Horne Fisher himself who sat in a corner, lowering over the fire.

"We jolly well have to thank him for putting some new life into the old party," Ashton Fisher was saying. "This campaign against the old squires just hits the degree of democracy there is in this county. This act for extending county council control is practically his bill; so you may say he's in the government even before he's in the House."

"One's easier than the other," said Harry, carelessly. "I bet the squire's a bigger pot than the county council in that county. Verner is pretty well rooted; all these rural places are what you call reactionary. Damning aristocrats won't alter it."

"He damns them rather well," observed Ashton. "We never had a better meeting than the one in Barkington, which generally goes Constitutional. And when he said, 'Sir Francis may boast of blue blood; let us show we have red blood,' and went on to talk about manhood and liberty, the room simply rose at him."

"Speaks very well," said Lord Saltoun, gruffly, making his only contribution to the conversation so far.

Then the almost equally silent Horne Fisher suddenly spoke, without taking his brooding eyes off the fire.

"What I can't understand," he said, "is why nobody is ever slanged for the real reason."

"Hullo!" remarked Harry, humorously, "you beginning to take notice?"

"Well, take Verner," continued Horne Fisher. "If we want to attack Verner, why not attack him? Why compliment him on being a romantic reactionary aristocrat? Who is Verner? Where does he come from? His name sounds old, but I never heard of it before, as the man said of the Crucifixion. Why talk about his blue blood? His blood may be gamboge yellow with green spots, for all anybody knows. All we know is that the old squire, Hawker, somehow ran through his money (and his second wife's, I suppose, for she was rich enough), and sold the estate to a man named Verner. What did he make his money in? Oil? Army contracts?"

"I don't know," said Saltoun, looking at him thoughtfully.

"First thing I ever knew you didn't know," cried the exuberant

Harry.

"And there's more, besides," went on Horne Fisher, who seemed to have suddenly found his tongue. "If we want country people to vote for us, why don't we get somebody with some notion about the country? We don't talk to people in Threadneedle Street about nothing but turnips and pigsties. Why do we talk to people in Somerset about nothing but slums and socialism? Why don't we give the squire's land to the squire's tenants, instead of dragging in the county council?"

"Three acres and a cow," cried Harry, emitting what the

Parliamentary reports call an ironical cheer.

"Yes," replied his brother, stubbornly. "Don't you think agricultural laborers would rather have three acres and a cow than three acres of printed forms and a committee? Why doesn't somebody start a yeoman party in politics, appealing to the old traditions of the small landowner? And why don't they attack men like Verner for what they are, which is something about as old and traditional as an American oil trust?"

"You'd better lead the yeoman party yourself," laughed Harry.

"Don't you think it would be a joke, Lord Saltoun, to see my brother

and his merry men, with their bows and bills, marching down to

Somerset all in Lincoln green instead of Lincoln and Bennet hats?"

"No," answered Old Saltoun, "I don't think it would be a joke. I think it would be an exceedingly serious and sensible idea."

"Well, I'm jiggered!" cried Harry Fisher, staring at him. "I said just now it was the first fact you didn't know, and I should say this is the first joke you didn't see."

"I've seen a good many things in my time," said the old man, in his rather sour fashion. "I've told a good many lies in my time, too, and perhaps I've got rather sick of them. But there are lies and lies, for all that. Gentlemen used to lie just as schoolboys lie, because they hung together and partly to help one another out. But I'm damned if I can see why we should lie for these cosmopolitan cads who only help themselves. They're not backing us up any more; they're simply crowding us out. If a man like your brother likes to go into Parliament as a yeoman or a gentleman or a Jacobite or an Ancient Briton, I should say it would be a jolly good thing."

In the rather startled silence that followed Horne Fisher sprang to his feet and all his dreary manner dropped off him.

"I'm ready to do it to-morrow," he cried. "I suppose none of you fellows would back me up."

Then Harry Fisher showed the finer side of his impetuosity. He made a sudden movement as if to shake hands.

"You're a sport," he said, "and I'll back you up, if nobody else will. But we can all back you up, can't we? I see what Lord Saltoun means, and, of course, he's right. He's always right."

"So I will go down to Somerset," said Horne Fisher.

"Yes, it is on the way to Westminster," said Lord Saltoun, with a smile.

And so it happened that Horne Fisher arrived some days later at the little station of a rather remote market town in the west, accompanied by a light suitcase and a lively brother. It must not be supposed, however, that the brother's cheerful tone consisted entirely of chaff. He supported the new candidate with hope as well as hilarity; and at the back of his boisterous partnership there was an increasing sympathy and encouragement. Harry Fisher had always had an affection for his more quiet and eccentric brother, and was now coming more and more to have a respect for him. As the campaign proceeded the respect increased to ardent admiration. For Harry was still young, and could feel the sort of enthusiasm for his captain in electioneering that a schoolboy can feel for his captain in cricket.

Nor was the admiration undeserved. As the new three-cornered contest developed it became apparent to others besides his devoted kinsman that there was more in Horne Fisher than had ever met the eye. It was clear that his outbreak by the family fireside had been but the culmination of a long course of brooding and studying on the question. The talent he retained through life for studying his subject, and even somebody else's subject, had long been concentrated on this idea of championing a new peasantry against a new plutocracy. He spoke to a crowd with eloquence and replied to an individual with humor, two political arts that seemed to come to him naturally. He certainly knew much more about rural problems than either Hughes, the Reform candidate, or Verner, the Constitutional candidate. And he probed those problems with a human curiosity, and went below the surface in a way that neither of them dreamed of doing. He soon became the voice of popular feelings that are never found in the popular press. New angles of criticism, arguments that had never before been uttered by an educated voice, tests and comparisons that had been made only in dialect by men drinking in the little local public houses, crafts half forgotten that had come down by sign of hand and tongue from remote ages when their fathers were free—all this created a curious and double excitement. It startled the well informed by being a new and fantastic idea they had never encountered. It startled the ignorant by being an old and familiar idea they never thought to have seen revived. Men saw things in a new light, and knew not even whether it was the sunset or the dawn.

Practical grievances were there to make the movement formidable. As Fisher went to and fro among the cottages and country inns, it was borne in on him without difficulty that Sir Francis Verner was a very bad landlord. Nor was the story of his acquisition of the land any more ancient and dignified than he had supposed; the story was well known in the county and in most respects was obvious enough. Hawker, the old squire, had been a loose, unsatisfactory sort of person, had been on bad terms with his first wife (who died, as some said, of neglect), and had then married a flashy South American Jewess with a fortune. But he must have worked his way through this fortune also with marvelous rapidity, for he had been compelled to sell the estate to Verner and had gone to live in South America, possibly on his wife's estates. But Fisher noticed that the laxity of the old squire was far less hated than the efficiency of the new squire. Verner's history seemed to be full of smart bargains and financial flutters that left other people short of money and temper. But though he heard a great deal about Verner, there was one thing that continually eluded him; something that nobody knew, that even Saltoun had not known. He could not find out how Verner had originally made his money.

"He must have kept it specially dark," said Horne Fisher to himself. "It must be something he's really ashamed of. Hang it all! what is a man ashamed of nowadays?"

And as he pondered on the possibilities they grew darker and more distorted in his mind; he thought vaguely of things remote and repulsive, strange forms of slavery or sorcery, and then of ugly things yet more unnatural but nearer home. The figure of Verner seemed to be blackened and transfigured in his imagination, and to stand against varied backgrounds and strange skies.

As he strode up a village street, brooding thus, his eyes encountered a complete contrast in the face of his other rival, the Reform candidate. Eric Hughes, with his blown blond hair and eager undergraduate face, was just getting into his motor car and saying a few final words to his agent, a sturdy, grizzled man named Gryce. Eric Hughes waved his hand in a friendly fashion; but Gryce eyed him with some hostility. Eric Hughes was a young man with genuine political enthusiasms, but he knew that political opponents are people with whom one may have to dine any day. But Mr. Gryce was a grim little local Radical, a champion of the chapel, and one of those happy people whose work is also their hobby. He turned his back as the motor car drove away, and walked briskly up the sunlit high street of the little town, whistling, with political papers sticking out of his pocket.

Fisher looked pensively after the resolute figure for a moment, and then, as if by an impulse, began to follow it. Through the busy market place, amid the baskets and barrows of market day, under the painted wooden sign of the Green Dragon, up a dark side entry, under an arch, and through a tangle of crooked cobbled streets the two threaded their way, the square, strutting figure in front and the lean, lounging figure behind him, like his shadow in the sunshine. At length they came to a brown brick house with a brass plate, on which was Mr. Gryce's name, and that individual turned and beheld his pursuer with a stare.

"Could I have a word with you, sir?" asked Horne Fisher, politely. The agent stared still more, but assented civilly, and led the other into an office littered with leaflets and hung all round with highly colored posters which linked the name of Hughes with all the higher interests of humanity.

"Mr. Horne Fisher, I believe," said Mr. Gryce. "Much honored by the call, of course. Can't pretend to congratulate you on entering the contest, I'm afraid; you won't expect that. Here we've been keeping the old flag flying for freedom and reform, and you come in and break the battle line."

For Mr. Elijah Gryce abounded in military metaphors and in denunciations of militarism. He was a square-jawed, blunt-featured man with a pugnacious cock of the eyebrow. He had been pickled in the politics of that countryside from boyhood, he knew everybody's secrets, and electioneering was the romance of his life.

"I suppose you think I'm devoured with ambition," said Horne Fisher, in his rather listless voice, "aiming at a dictatorship and all that. Well, I think I can clear myself of the charge of mere selfish ambition. I only want certain things done. I don't want to do them. I very seldom want to do anything. And I've come here to say that I'm quite willing to retire from the contest if you can convince me that we really want to do the same thing."

The agent of the Reform party looked at him with an odd and slightly puzzled expression, and before he could reply, Fisher went on in the same level tones:

"You'd hardly believe it, but I keep a conscience concealed about me; and I am in doubt about several things. For instance, we both want to turn Verner out of Parliament, but what weapon are we to use? I've heard a lot of gossip against him, but is it right to act on mere gossip? Just as I want to be fair to you, so I want to be fair to him. If some of the things I've heard are true he ought to be turned out of Parliament and every other club in London. But I don't want to turn him out of Parliament if they aren't true."

At this point the light of battle sprang into Mr. Gryce's eyes and he became voluble, not to say violent. He, at any rate, had no doubt that the stories were true; he could testify, to his own knowledge, that they were true. Verner was not only a hard landlord, but a mean landlord, a robber as well as a rackrenter; any gentleman would be justified in hounding him out. He had cheated old Wilkins out of his freehold by a trick fit for a pickpocket; he had driven old Mother Biddle to the workhouse; he had stretched the law against Long Adam, the poacher, till all the magistrates were ashamed of him.

"So if you'll serve under the old banner," concluded Mr. Gryce, more genially, "and turn out a swindling tyrant like that, I'm sure you'll never regret it."

"And if that is the truth," said Horne Fisher, "are you going to tell it?"

"What do you mean? Tell the truth?" demanded Gryce.

"I mean you are going to tell the truth as you have just told it," replied Fisher. "You are going to placard this town with the wickedness done to old Wilkins. You are going to fill the newspapers with the infamous story of Mrs. Biddle. You are going to denounce Verner from a public platform, naming him for what he did and naming the poacher he did it to. And you're going to find out by what trade this man made the money with which he bought the estate; and when you know the truth, as I said before, of course you are going to tell it. Upon those terms I come under the old flag, as you call it, and haul down my little pennon."

The agent was eying him with a curious expression, surly but not entirely unsympathetic. "Well," he said, slowly, "you have to do these things in a regular way, you know, or people don't understand. I've had a lot of experience, and I'm afraid what you say wouldn't do. People understand slanging squires in a general way, but those personalities aren't considered fair play. Looks like hitting below the belt."

"Old Wilkins hasn't got a belt, I suppose," replied Horne Fisher. "Verner can hit him anyhow, and nobody must say a word. It's evidently very important to have a belt. But apparently you have to be rather high up in society to have one. Possibly," he added, thoughtfully—"possibly the explanation of the phrase 'a belted earl,' the meaning of which has always escaped me."

"I mean those personalities won't do," returned Gryce, frowning at the table.

"And Mother Biddle and Long Adam, the poacher, are not personalities," said Fisher, "and suppose we mustn't ask how Verner made all the money that enabled him to become—a personality."

Gryce was still looking at him under lowering brows, but the singular light in his eyes had brightened. At last he said, in another and much quieter voice:

"Look here, sir. I like you, if you don't mind my saying so. I think you are really on the side of the people and I'm sure you're a brave man. A lot braver than you know, perhaps. We daren't touch what you propose with a barge pole; and so far from wanting you in the old party, we'd rather you ran your own risk by yourself. But because I like you and respect your pluck, I'll do you a good turn before we part. I don't want you to waste time barking up the wrong tree. You talk about how the new squire got the money to buy, and the ruin of the old squire, and all the rest of it. Well, I'll give you a hint about that, a hint about something precious few people know."

"I am very grateful," said Fisher, gravely. "What is it?"

"It's in two words," said the other. "The new squire was quite poor when he bought. The old squire was quite rich when he sold."

Horne Fisher looked at him thoughtfully as he turned away abruptly and busied himself with the papers on his desk. Then Fisher uttered a short phrase of thanks and farewell, and went out into the street, still very thoughtful.

His reflection seemed to end in resolution, and, falling into a more rapid stride, he passed out of the little town along a road leading toward the gate of the great park, the country seat of Sir Francis Verner. A glitter of sunlight made the early winter more like a late autumn, and the dark woods were touched here and there with red and golden leaves, like the last rays of a lost sunset. From a higher part of the road he had seen the long, classical facade of the great house with its many windows, almost immediately beneath him, but when the road ran down under the wall of the estate, topped with towering trees behind, he realized that it was half a mile round to the lodge gates. After walking for a few minutes along the lane, however, he came to a place where the wall had cracked and was in process of repair. As it was, there was a great gap in the gray masonry that looked at first as black as a cavern and only showed at a second glance the twilight of the twinkling trees. There was something fascinating about that unexpected gate, like the opening of a fairy tale.

Horne Fisher had in him something of the aristocrat, which is very near to the anarchist. It was characteristic of him that he turned into this dark and irregular entry as casually as into his own front door, merely thinking that it would be a short cut to the house. He made his way through the dim wood for some distance and with some difficulty, until there began to shine through the trees a level light, in lines of silver, which he did not at first understand. The next moment he had come out into the daylight at the top of a steep bank, at the bottom of which a path ran round the rim of a large ornamental lake. The sheet of water which he had seen shimmering through the trees was of considerable extent, but was walled in on every side with woods which were not only dark, but decidedly dismal. At one end of the path was a classical statue of some nameless nymph, and at the other end it was flanked by two classical urns; but the marble was weather-stained and streaked with green and gray. A hundred other signs, smaller but more significant, told him that he had come on some outlying corner of the grounds neglected and seldom visited. In the middle of the lake was what appeared to be an island, and on the island what appeared to be meant for a classical temple, not open like a temple of the winds, but with a blank wall between its Doric pillars. We may say it only seemed like an island, because a second glance revealed a low causeway of flat stones running up to it from the shore and turning it into a peninsula. And certainly it only seemed like a temple, for nobody knew better than Horne Fisher that no god had ever dwelt in that shrine.

"That's what makes all this classical landscape gardening so desolate," he said to himself. "More desolate than Stonehenge or the Pyramids. We don't believe in Egyptian mythology, but the Egyptians did; and I suppose even the Druids believed in Druidism. But the eighteenth-century gentleman who built these temples didn't believe in Venus or Mercury any more than we do; that's why the reflection of those pale pillars in the lake is truly only the shadow of a shade. They were men of the age of Reason; they, who filled their gardens with these stone nymphs, had less hope than any men in all history of really meeting a nymph in the forest."

His monologue stopped abruptly with a sharp noise like a thundercrack that rolled in dreary echoes round the dismal mere. He knew at once what it was—somebody had fired off a gun. But as to the meaning of it he was momentarily staggered, and strange thoughts thronged into his mind. The next moment he laughed; for he saw lying a little way along the path below him the dead bird that the shot had brought down.

At the same moment, however, he saw something else, which interested him more. A ring of dense trees ran round the back of the island temple, framing the facade of it in dark foliage, and he could have sworn he saw a stir as of something moving among the leaves. The next moment his suspicion was confirmed, for a rather ragged figure came from under the shadow of the temple and began to move along the causeway that led to the bank. Even at that distance the figure was conspicuous by its great height and Fisher could see that the man carried a gun under his arm. There came back into his memory at once the name Long Adam, the poacher.

With a rapid sense of strategy he sometimes showed, Fisher sprang from the bank and raced round the lake to the head of the little pier of stones. If once a man reached the mainland he could easily vanish into the woods. But when Fisher began to advance along the stones toward the island, the man was cornered in a blind alley and could only back toward the temple. Putting his broad shoulders against it, he stood as if at bay; he was a comparatively young man, with fine lines in his lean face and figure and a mop of ragged red hair. The look in his eyes might well have been disquieting to anyone left alone with him on an island in the middle of a lake.

"Good morning," said Horne Fisher, pleasantly. "I thought at first you were a murderer. But it seems unlikely, somehow, that the partridge rushed between us and died for love of me, like the heroines in the romances; so I suppose you are a poacher."

"I suppose you would call me a poacher," answered the man; and his voice was something of a surprise coming from such a scarecrow; it had that hard fastidiousness to be found in those who have made a fight for their own refinement among rough surroundings. "I consider I have a perfect right to shoot game in this place. But I am well aware that people of your sort take me for a thief, and I suppose you will try to land me in jail."

"There are preliminary difficulties," replied Fisher. "To begin with, the mistake is flattering, but I am not a gamekeeper. Still less am I three gamekeepers, who would be, I imagine, about your fighting weight. But I confess I have another reason for not wanting to jail you."

"And what is that?" asked the other.

"Only that I quite agree with you," answered Fisher. "I don't exactly say you have a right to poach, but I never could see that it was as wrong as being a thief. It seems to me against the whole normal notion of property that a man should own something because it flies across his garden. He might as well own the wind, or think he could write his name on a morning cloud. Besides, if we want poor people to respect property we must give them some property to respect. You ought to have land of your own; and I'm going to give you some if I can."

"Going to give me some land!" repeated Long Adam.

"I apologize for addressing you as if you were a public meeting," said Fisher, "but I am an entirely new kind of public man who says the same thing in public and in private. I've said this to a hundred huge meetings throughout the country, and I say it to you on this queer little island in this dismal pond. I would cut up a big estate like this into small estates for everybody, even for poachers. I would do in England as they did in Ireland—buy the big men out, if possible; get them out, anyhow. A man like you ought to have a little place of his own. I don't say you could keep pheasants, but you might keep chickens."

The man stiffened suddenly and he seemed at once to blanch and flame at the promise as if it were a threat.

"Chickens!" he repeated, with a passion of contempt.

"Why do you object?" asked the placid candidate. "Because keeping hens is rather a mild amusement for a poacher? What about poaching eggs?"

"Because I am not a poacher," cried Adam, in a rending voice that rang round the hollow shrines and urns like the echoes of his gun. "Because the partridge lying dead over there is my partridge. Because the land you are standing on is my land. Because my own land was only taken from me by a crime, and a worse crime than poaching. This has been a single estate for hundreds and hundreds of years, and if you or any meddlesome mountebank comes here and talks of cutting it up like a cake, if I ever hear a word more of you and your leveling lies—"

"You seem to be a rather turbulent public," observed Horne Fisher, "but do go on. What will happen if I try to divide this estate decently among decent people?"

The poacher had recovered a grim composure as he replied. "There will be no partridge to rush in between."

With that he turned his back, evidently resolved to say no more, and walked past the temple to the extreme end of the islet, where he stood staring into the water. Fisher followed him, but, when his repeated questions evoked no answer, turned back toward the shore. In doing so he took a second and closer look at the artificial temple, and noted some curious things about it. Most of these theatrical things were as thin as theatrical scenery, and he expected the classic shrine to be a shallow thing, a mere shell or mask. But there was some substantial bulk of it behind, buried in the trees, which had a gray, labyrinthian look, like serpents of stone, and lifted a load of leafy towers to the sky. But what arrested Fisher's eye was that in this bulk of gray-white stone behind there was a single door with great, rusty bolts outside; the bolts, however, were not shot across so as to secure it. Then he walked round the small building, and found no other opening except one small grating like a ventilator, high up in the wall. He retraced his steps thoughtfully along the causeway to the banks of the lake, and sat down on the stone steps between the two sculptured funeral urns. Then he lit a cigarette and smoked it in ruminant manner; eventually he took out a notebook and wrote down various phrases, numbering and renumbering them till they stood in the following order: "(1) Squire Hawker disliked his first wife. (2) He married his second wife for her money. (3) Long Adam says the estate is really his. (4) Long Adam hangs round the island temple, which looks like a prison. (5) Squire Hawker was not poor when he gave up the estate. (6) Verner was poor when he got the estate."

He gazed at these notes with a gravity which gradually turned to a hard smile, threw away his cigarette, and resumed his search for a short cut to the great house. He soon picked up the path which, winding among clipped hedges and flower beds, brought him in front of its long Palladian facade. It had the usual appearance of being, not a private house, but a sort of public building sent into exile in the provinces.

He first found himself in the presence of the butler, who really looked much older than the building, for the architecture was dated as Georgian; but the man's face, under a highly unnatural brown wig, was wrinkled with what might have been centuries. Only his prominent eyes were alive and alert, as if with protest. Fisher glanced at him, and then stopped and said:

"Excuse me. Weren't you with the late squire, Mr. Hawker?"

"Yes, sir," said the man, gravely. "Usher is my name. What can I do for you?"

"Only take me into Sir Francis Verner," replied the visitor.

Sir Francis Verner was sitting in an easy chair beside a small table in a large room hung with tapestries. On the table were a small flask and glass, with the green glimmer of a liqueur and a cup of black coffee. He was clad in a quiet gray suit with a moderately harmonious purple tie; but Fisher saw something about the turn of his fair mustache and the lie of his flat hair—it suddenly revealed that his name was Franz Werner.

"You are Mr. Horne Fisher," he said. "Won't you sit down?"

"No, thank you," replied Fisher. "I fear this is not a friendly occasion, and I shall remain standing. Possibly you know that I am already standing—standing for Parliament, in fact—"

"I am aware we are political opponents," replied Verner, raising his eyebrows. "But I think it would be better if we fought in a sporting spirit; in a spirit of English fair play."

"Much better," assented Fisher. "It would be much better if you were English and very much better if you had ever played fair. But what I've come to say can be said very shortly. I don't quite know how we stand with the law about that old Hawker story, but my chief object is to prevent England being entirely ruled by people like you. So whatever the law would say, I will say no more if you will retire from the election at once."

"You are evidently a lunatic," said Verner.

"My psychology may be a little abnormal," replied Horne Fisher, in a rather hazy manner. "I am subject to dreams, especially day-dreams. Sometimes what is happening to me grows vivid in a curious double way, as if it had happened before. Have you ever had that mystical feeling that things have happened before?"

"I hope you are a harmless lunatic," said Verner.

But Fisher was still staring in an absent fashion at the golden gigantic figures and traceries of brown and red in the tapestries on the walls; then he looked again at Verner and resumed: "I have a feeling that this interview has happened before, here in this tapestried room, and we are two ghosts revisiting a haunted chamber. But it was Squire Hawker who sat where you sit and it was you who stood where I stand." He paused a moment and then added, with simplicity, "I suppose I am a blackmailer, too."

"If you are," said Sir Francis, "I promise you you shall go to jail." But his face had a shade on it that looked like the reflection of the green wine gleaming on the table. Horne Fisher regarded him steadily and answered, quietly enough:

"Blackmailers do not always go to jail. Sometimes they go to Parliament. But, though Parliament is rotten enough already, you shall not go there if I can help it. I am not so criminal as you were in bargaining with crime. You made a squire give up his country seat. I only ask you to give up your Parliamentary seat."

Sir Francis Verner sprang to his feet and looked about for one of the bell ropes of the old-fashioned, curtained room.

"Where is Usher?" he cried, with a livid face.

"And who is Usher?" said Fisher, softly. "I wonder how much Usher knows of the truth."

Verner's hand fell from the bell rope and, after standing for a moment with rolling eyes, he strode abruptly from the room. Fisher went but by the other door, by which he had entered, and, seeing no sign of Usher, let himself out and betook himself again toward the town.

That night he put an electric torch in his pocket and set out alone in the darkness to add the last links to his argument. There was much that he did not know yet; but he thought he knew where he could find the knowledge. The night closed dark and stormy and the black gap in the wall looked blacker than ever; the wood seemed to have grown thicker and darker in a day. If the deserted lake with its black woods and gray urns and images looked desolate even by daylight, under the night and the growing storm it seemed still more like the pool of Acheron in the land of lost souls. As he stepped carefully along the jetty stones he seemed to be traveling farther and farther into the abyss of night, and to have left behind him the last points from which it would be possible to signal to the land of the living. The lake seemed to have grown larger than a sea, but a sea of black and slimy waters that slept with abominable serenity, as if they had washed out the world. There was so much of this nightmare sense of extension and expansion that he was strangely surprised to come to his desert island so soon. But he knew it for a place of inhuman silence and solitude; and he felt as if he had been walking for years.

Nerving himself to a more normal mood, he paused under one of the dark dragon trees that branched out above him, and, taking out his torch, turned in the direction of the door at the back of the temple. It was unbolted as before, and the thought stirred faintly in him that it was slightly open, though only by a crack. The more he thought of it, however, the more certain he grew that this was but one of the common illusions of light coming from a different angle. He studied in a more scientific spirit the details of the door, with its rusty bolts and hinges, when he became conscious of something very near him—indeed, nearly above his head. Something was dangling from the tree that was not a broken branch. For some seconds he stood as still as a stone, and as cold. What he saw above him were the legs of a man hanging, presumably a dead man hanged. But the next moment he knew better. The man was literally alive and kicking; and an instant after he had dropped to the ground and turned on the intruder. Simultaneously three or four other trees seemed to come to life in the same fashion. Five or six other figures had fallen on their feet from these unnatural nests. It was as if the place were an island of monkeys. But a moment after they had made a stampede toward him, and when they laid their hands on him he knew that they were men.

With the electric torch in his hand he struck the foremost of them so furiously in the face that the man stumbled and rolled over on the slimy grass; but the torch was broken and extinguished, leaving everything in a denser obscurity. He flung another man flat against the temple wall, so that he slid to the ground; but a third and fourth carried Fisher off his feet and began to bear him, struggling, toward the doorway. Even in the bewilderment of the battle he was conscious that the door was standing open. Somebody was summoning the roughs from inside.

The moment they were within they hurled him upon a sort of bench or bed with violence, but no damage; for the settee, or whatever it was, seemed to be comfortably cushioned for his reception. Their violence had in it a great element of haste, and before he could rise they had all rushed for the door to escape. Whatever bandits they were that infested this desert island, they were obviously uneasy about their job and very anxious to be quit of it. He had the flying fancy that regular criminals would hardly be in such a panic. The next moment the great door crashed to and he could hear the bolts shriek as they shot into their place, and the feet of the retreating men scampering and stumbling along the causeway. But rapidly as it happened, it did not happen before Fisher had done something that he wanted to do. Unable to rise from his sprawling attitude in that flash of time, he had shot out one of his long legs and hooked it round the ankle of the last man disappearing through the door. The man swayed and toppled over inside the prison chamber, and the door closed between him and his fleeing companions. Clearly they were in too much haste to realize that they had left one of their company behind.

The man sprang to his feet again and hammered and kicked furiously at the door. Fisher's sense of humor began to recover from the struggle and he sat up on his sofa with something of his native nonchalance. But as he listened to the captive captor beating on the door of the prison, a new and curious reflection came to him.

The natural course for a man thus wishing to attract his friends' attention would be to call out, to shout as well as kick. This man was making as much noise as he could with his feet and hands, but not a sound came from his throat. Why couldn't he speak? At first he thought the man might be gagged, which was manifestly absurd. Then his fancy fell back on the ugly idea that the man was dumb. He hardly knew why it was so ugly an idea, but it affected his imagination in a dark and disproportionate fashion. There seemed to be something creepy about the idea of being left in a dark room with a deaf mute. It was almost as if such a defect were a deformity. It was almost as if it went with other and worse deformities. It was as if the shape he could not trace in the darkness were some shape that should not see the sun.

Then he had a flash of sanity and also of insight. The explanation was very simple, but rather interesting. Obviously the man did not use his voice because he did not wish his voice to be recognized. He hoped to escape from that dark place before Fisher found out who he was. And who was he? One thing at least was clear. He was one or other of the four or five men with whom Fisher had already talked in these parts, and in the development of that strange story.

"Now I wonder who you are," he said, aloud, with all his old lazy urbanity. "I suppose it's no use trying to throttle you in order to find out; it would be displeasing to pass the night with a corpse. Besides I might be the corpse. I've got no matches and I've smashed my torch, so I can only speculate. Who could you be, now? Let us think."

The man thus genially addressed had desisted from drumming on the door and retreated sullenly into a corner as Fisher continued to address him in a flowing monologue.

"Probably you are the poacher who says he isn't a poacher. He says he's a landed proprietor; but he will permit me to inform him that, whatever he is, he's a fool. What hope can there ever be of a free peasantry in England if the peasants themselves are such snobs as to want to be gentlemen? How can we make a democracy with no democrats? As it is, you want to be a landlord and so you consent to be a criminal. And in that, you know, you are rather like somebody else. And, now I think of it, perhaps you are somebody else."

There was a silence broken by breathing from the corner and the murmur of the rising storm, that came in through the small grating above the man's head. Horne Fisher continued:

"Are you only a servant, perhaps, that rather sinister old servant who was butler to Hawker and Verner? If so, you are certainly the only link between the two periods. But if so, why do you degrade yourself to serve this dirty foreigner, when you at least saw the last of a genuine national gentry? People like you are generally at least patriotic. Doesn't England mean anything to you, Mr. Usher? All of which eloquence is possibly wasted, as perhaps you are not Mr. Usher.

"More likely you are Verner himself; and it's no good wasting eloquence to make you ashamed of yourself. Nor is it any good to curse you for corrupting England; nor are you the right person to curse. It is the English who deserve to be cursed, and are cursed, because they allowed such vermin to crawl into the high places of their heroes and their kings. I won't dwell on the idea that you're Verner, or the throttling might begin, after all. Is there anyone else you could be? Surely you're not some servant of the other rival organization. I can't believe you're Gryce, the agent; and yet Gryce had a spark of the fanatic in his eye, too; and men will do extraordinary things in these paltry feuds of politics. Or if not the servant, is it the . . . No, I can't believe it . . . not the red blood of manhood and liberty . . . not the democratic ideal . . ."

He sprang up in excitement, and at the same moment a growl of thunder came through the grating beyond. The storm had broken, and with it a new light broke on his mind. There was something else that might happen in a moment.

"Do you know what that means?" he cried. "It means that God himself may hold a candle to show me your infernal face."

Then next moment came a crash of thunder; but before the thunder a white light had filled the whole room for a single split second.

Fisher had seen two things in front of him. One was the black-and-white pattern of the iron grating against the sky; the other was the face in the corner. It was the face of his brother.

Nothing came from Horne Fisher's lips except a Christian name, which was followed by a silence more dreadful than the dark. At last the other figure stirred and sprang up, and the voice of Harry Fisher was heard for the first time in that horrible room.

"You've seen me, I suppose," he said, "and we may as well have a light now. You could have turned it on at any time, if you'd found the switch."

He pressed a button in the wall and all the details of that room sprang into something stronger than daylight. Indeed, the details were so unexpected that for a moment they turned the captive's rocking mind from the last personal revelation. The room, so far from being a dungeon cell, was more like a drawing-room, even a lady's drawing-room, except for some boxes of cigars and bottles of wine that were stacked with books and magazines on a side table. A second glance showed him that the more masculine fittings were quite recent, and that the more feminine background was quite old. His eye caught a strip of faded tapestry, which startled him into speech, to the momentary oblivion of bigger matters.

"This place was furnished from the great house," he said.

"Yes," replied the other, "and I think you know why."

"I think I do," said Horne Fisher, "and before I go on to more extraordinary things I will, say what I think. Squire Hawker played both the bigamist and the bandit. His first wife was not dead when he married the Jewess; she was imprisoned on this island. She bore him a child here, who now haunts his birthplace under the name of Long Adam. A bankruptcy company promoter named Werner discovered the secret and blackmailed the squire into surrendering the estate. That's all quite clear and very easy. And now let me go on to something more difficult. And that is for you to explain what the devil you are doing kidnaping your born brother."

After a pause Henry Fisher answered:

"I suppose you didn't expect to see me," he said. "But, after all, what could you expect?'"

"I'm afraid I don't follow," said Horne Fisher.

"I mean what else could you expect, after making such a muck of it?" said his brother, sulkily. "We all thought you were so clever. How could we know you were going to be—well, really, such a rotten failure?"

"This is rather curious," said the candidate, frowning. "Without vanity, I was not under the impression that my candidature was a failure. All the big meetings were successful and crowds of people have promised me votes."

"I should jolly well think they had," said Henry, grimly. "You've made a landslide with your confounded acres and a cow, and Verner can hardly get a vote anywhere. Oh, it's too rotten for anything!"

"What on earth do you mean?"

"Why, you lunatic," cried Henry, in tones of ringing sincerity, "you don't suppose you were meant to win the seat, did you? Oh, it's too childish! I tell you Verner's got to get in. Of course he's got to get in. He's to have the Exchequer next session, and there's the Egyptian loan and Lord knows what else. We only wanted you to split the Reform vote because accidents might happen after Hughes had made a score at Barkington."

"I see," said Fisher, "and you, I think, are a pillar and ornament of the Reform party. As you say, I am not clever."

The appeal to party loyalty fell on deaf ears; for the pillar of Reform was brooding on other things. At last he said, in a more troubled voice:

"I didn't want you to catch me; I knew it would be a shock. But I tell you what, you never would have caught me if I hadn't come here myself, to see they didn't ill treat you and to make sure everything was as comfortable as it could be." There was even a sort of break in his voice as he added, "I got those cigars because I knew you liked them."

Emotions are queer things, and the idiocy of this concession suddenly softened Horne Fisher like an unfathomable pathos.

"Never mind, old chap," he said; "we'll say no more about it. I'll admit that you're really as kind-hearted and affectionate a scoundrel and hypocrite as ever sold himself to ruin his country. There, I can't say handsomer than that. Thank you for the cigars, old man. I'll have one if you don't mind."

By the time that Horne Fisher had ended his telling of this story to Harold March they had come out into one of the public parks and taken a seat on a rise of ground overlooking wide green spaces under a blue and empty sky; and there was something incongruous in the words with which the narration ended.

"I have been in that room ever since," said Horne Fisher. "I am in it now. I won the election, but I never went to the House. My life has been a life in that little room on that lonely island. Plenty of books and cigars and luxuries, plenty of knowledge and interest and information, but never a voice out of that tomb to reach the world outside. I shall probably die there." And he smiled as he looked across the vast green park to the gray horizon.

VIII. THE VENGEANCE OF THE STATUE

It was on the sunny veranda of a seaside hotel, overlooking a pattern of flower beds and a strip of blue sea, that Horne Fisher and Harold March had their final explanation, which might be called an explosion.

Harold March had come to the little table and sat down at it with a subdued excitement smoldering in his somewhat cloudy and dreamy blue eyes. In the newspapers which he tossed from him on to the table there was enough to explain some if not all of his emotion. Public affairs in every department had reached a crisis. The government which had stood so long that men were used to it, as they are used to a hereditary despotism, had begun to be accused of blunders and even of financial abuses. Some said that the experiment of attempting to establish a peasantry in the west of England, on the lines of an early fancy of Horne Fisher's, had resulted in nothing but dangerous quarrels with more industrial neighbors. There had been particular complaints of the ill treatment of harmless foreigners, chiefly Asiatics, who happened to be employed in the new scientific works constructed on the coast. Indeed, the new Power which had arisen in Siberia, backed by Japan and other powerful allies, was inclined to take the matter up in the interests of its exiled subjects; and there had been wild talk about ambassadors and ultimatums. But something much more serious, in its personal interest for March himself, seemed to fill his meeting with his friend with a mixture of embarrassment and indignation.

Perhaps it increased his annoyance that there was a certain unusual liveliness about the usually languid figure of Fisher. The ordinary image of him in March's mind was that of a pallid and bald-browed gentleman, who seemed to be prematurely old as well as prematurely bald. He was remembered as a man who expressed the opinions of a pessimist in the language of a lounger. Even now March could not be certain whether the change was merely a sort of masquerade of sunshine, or that effect of clear colors and clean-cut outlines that is always visible on the parade of a marine resort, relieved against the blue dado of the sea. But Fisher had a flower in his buttonhole, and his friend could have sworn he carried his cane with something almost like the swagger of a fighter. With such clouds gathering over England, the pessimist seemed to be the only man who carried his own sunshine.

"Look here," said Harold March, abruptly, "you've been no end of a friend to me, and I never was so proud of a friendship before; but there's something I must get off my chest. The more I found out, the less I understood how you could stand it. And I tell you I'm going to stand it no longer."

Horne Fisher gazed across at him gravely and attentively, but rather as if he were a long way off.

"You know I always liked you," said Fisher, quietly, "but I also respect you, which is not always the same thing. You may possibly guess that I like a good many people I don't respect. Perhaps it is my tragedy, perhaps it is my fault. But you are very different, and I promise you this: that I will never try to keep you as somebody to be liked, at the price of your not being respected."

"I know you are magnanimous," said March after a silence, "and yet you tolerate and perpetuate everything that is mean." Then after another silence he added: "Do you remember when we first met, when you were fishing in that brook in the affair of the target? And do you remember you said that, after all, it might do no harm if I could blow the whole tangle of this society to hell with dynamite."

"Yes, and what of that?" asked Fisher.

"Only that I'm going to blow it to hell with dynamite," said Harold March, "and I think it right to give you fair warning. For a long time I didn't believe things were as bad as you said they were. But I never felt as if I could have bottled up what you knew, supposing you really knew it. Well, the long and the short of it is that I've got a conscience; and now, at last, I've also got a chance. I've been put in charge of a big independent paper, with a free hand, and we're going to open a cannonade on corruption."

"That will be—Attwood, I suppose," said Fisher, reflectively.

"Timber merchant. Knows a lot about China."

"He knows a lot about England," said March, doggedly, "and now I know it, too, we're not going to hush it up any longer. The people of this country have a right to know how they're ruled—or, rather, ruined. The Chancellor is in the pocket of the money lenders and has to do as he is told; otherwise he's bankrupt, and a bad sort of bankruptcy, too, with nothing but cards and actresses behind it. The Prime Minister was in the petrol-contract business; and deep in it, too. The Foreign Minister is a wreck of drink and drugs. When you say that plainly about a man who may send thousands of Englishmen to die for nothing, you're called personal. If a poor engine driver gets drunk and sends thirty or forty people to death, nobody complains of the exposure being personal. The engine driver is not a person."

"I quite agree with you," said Fisher, calmly. "You are perfectly right."

"If you agree with us, why the devil don't you act with us?" demanded his friend. "If you think it's right, why don't you do what's right? It's awful to think of a man of your abilities simply blocking the road to reform."

"We have often talked about that," replied Fisher, with the same composure. "The Prime Minister is my father's friend. The Foreign Minister married my sister. The Chancellor of the Exchequer is my first cousin. I mention the genealogy in some detail just now for a particular reason. The truth is I have a curious kind of cheerfulness at the moment. It isn't altogether the sun and the sea, sir. I am enjoying an emotion that is entirely new to me; a happy sensation I never remember having had before."

"What the devil do you mean?"

"I am feeling proud of my family," said Horne Fisher.

Harold March stared at him with round blue eyes, and seemed too much mystified even to ask a question. Fisher leaned back in his chair in his lazy fashion, and smiled as he continued.

"Look here, my dear fellow. Let me ask a question in turn. You imply that I have always known these things about my unfortunate kinsmen. So I have. Do you suppose that Attwood hasn't always known them? Do you suppose he hasn't always known you as an honest man who would say these things when he got a chance? Why does Attwood unmuzzle you like a dog at this moment, after all these years? I know why he does; I know a good many things, far too many things. And therefore, as I have the honor to remark, I am proud of my family at last."

"But why?" repeated March, rather feebly.

"I am proud of the Chancellor because he gambled and the Foreign Minister because he drank and the Prime Minister because he took a commission on a contract," said Fisher, firmly. "I am proud of them because they did these things, and can be denounced for them, and know they can be denounced for them, and are standing firm for all that. I take off my hat to them because they are defying blackmail, and refusing to smash their country to save themselves. I salute them as if they were going to die on the battlefield."

After a pause he continued: "And it will be a battlefield, too, and not a metaphorical one. We have yielded to foreign financiers so long that now it is war or ruin, Even the people, even the country people, are beginning to suspect that they are being ruined. That is the meaning of the regrettable incidents in the newspapers."

"The meaning of the outrages on Orientals?" asked March.

"The meaning of the outrages on Orientals," replied Fisher, "is that the financiers have introduced Chinese labor into this country with the deliberate intention of reducing workmen and peasants to starvation. Our unhappy politicians have made concession after concession; and now they are asking concessions which amount to our ordering a massacre of our own poor. If we do not fight now we shall never fight again. They will have put England in an economic position of starving in a week. But we are going to fight now; I shouldn't wonder if there were an ultimatum in a week and an invasion in a fortnight. All the past corruption and cowardice is hampering us, of course; the West country is pretty stormy and doubtful even in a military sense; and the Irish regiments there, that are supposed to support us by the new treaty, are pretty well in mutiny; for, of course, this infernal coolie capitalism is being pushed in Ireland, too. But it's to stop now; and if the government message of reassurance gets through to them in time, they may turn up after all by the time the enemy lands. For my poor old gang is going to stand to its guns at last. Of course it's only natural that when they have been whitewashed for half a century as paragons, their sins should come back on them at the very moment when they are behaving like men for the first time in their lives. Well, I tell you, March, I know them inside out; and I know they are behaving like heroes. Every man of them ought to have a statue, and on the pedestal words like those of the noblest ruffian of the Revolution: 'Que mon nom soit fletri; que la France soit libre.'"

"Good God!" cried March, "shall we never get to the bottom of your mines and countermines?"

After a silence Fisher answered in a lower voice, looking his friend in the eyes.

"Did you think there was nothing but evil at the bottom of them?" he asked, gently. "Did you think I had found nothing but filth in the deep seas into which fate has thrown me? Believe me, you never know the best about men till you know the worst about them. It does not dispose of their strange human souls to know that they were exhibited to the world as impossibly impeccable wax works, who never looked after a woman or knew the meaning of a bribe. Even in a palace, life can be lived well; and even in a Parliament, life can be lived with occasional efforts to live it well. I tell you it is as true of these rich fools and rascals as it is true of every poor footpad and pickpocket; that only God knows how good they have tried to be. God alone knows what the conscience can survive, or how a man who has lost his honor will still try to save his soul."

There was another silence, and March sat staring at the table and Fisher at the sea. Then Fisher suddenly sprang to his feet and caught up his hat and stick with all his new alertness and even pugnacity.

"Look here, old fellow," he cried, "let us make a bargain. Before you open your campaign for Attwood come down and stay with us for one week, to hear what we're really doing. I mean with the Faithful Few, formerly known as the Old Gang, occasionally to be described as the Low Lot. There are really only five of us that are quite fixed, and organizing the national defense; and we're living like a garrison in a sort of broken-down hotel in Kent. Come and see what we're really doing and what there is to be done, and do us justice. And after that, with unalterable love and affection for you, publish and be damned."

Thus it came about that in the last week before war, when events moved most rapidly, Harold March found himself one of a sort of small house party of the people he was proposing to denounce. They were living simply enough, for people with their tastes, in an old brown-brick inn faced with ivy and surrounded by rather dismal gardens. At the back of the building the garden ran up very steeply to a road along the ridge above; and a zigzag path scaled the slope in sharp angles, turning to and fro amid evergreens so somber that they might rather be called everblack. Here and there up the slope were statues having all the cold monstrosity of such minor ornaments of the eighteenth century; and a whole row of them ran as on a terrace along the last bank at the bottom, opposite the back door. This detail fixed itself first in March's mind merely because it figured in the first conversation he had with one of the cabinet ministers.

The cabinet ministers were rather older than he had expected to find them. The Prime Minister no longer looked like a boy, though he still looked a little like a baby. But it was one of those old and venerable babies, and the baby had soft gray hair. Everything about him was soft, to his speech and his way of walking; but over and above that his chief function seemed to be sleep. People left alone with him got so used to his eyes being closed that they were almost startled when they realized in the stillness that the eyes were wide open, and even watching. One thing at least would always make the old gentleman open his eyes. The one thing he really cared for in this world was his hobby of armored weapons, especially Eastern weapons, and he would talk for hours about Damascus blades and Arab swordmanship. Lord James Herries, the Chancellor of the Exchequer, was a short, dark, sturdy man with a very sallow face and a very sullen manner, which contrasted with the gorgeous flower in his buttonhole and his festive trick of being always slightly overdressed. It was something of a euphemism to call him a well-known man about town. There was perhaps more mystery in the question of how a man who lived for pleasure seemed to get so little pleasure out of it. Sir David Archer, the Foreign Secretary, was the only one of them who was a self-made man, and the only one of them who looked like an aristocrat. He was tall and thin and very handsome, with a grizzled beard; his gray hair was very curly, and even rose in front in two rebellious ringlets that seemed to the fanciful to tremble like the antennae of some giant insect, or to stir sympathetically with the restless tufted eyebrows over his rather haggard eyes. For the Foreign Secretary made no secret of his somewhat nervous condition, whatever might be the cause of it.

"Do you know that mood when one could scream because a mat is crooked?" he said to March, as they walked up and down in the back garden below the line of dingy statues. "Women get into it when they've worked too hard; and I've been working pretty hard lately, of course. It drives me mad when Herries will wear his hat a little crooked—habit of looking like a gay dog. Sometime I swear I'll knock it off. That statue of Britannia over there isn't quite straight; it sticks forward a bit as if the lady were going to topple over. The damned thing is that it doesn't topple over and be done with it. See, it's clamped with an iron prop. Don't be surprised if I get up in the middle of the night to hike it down."

They paced the path for a few moments in silence and then he continued. "It's odd those little things seem specially big when there are bigger things to worry about. We'd better go in and do some work."

Horne Fisher evidently allowed for all the neurotic possibilities of Archer and the dissipated habits of Herries; and whatever his faith in their present firmness, did not unduly tax their time and attention, even in the case of the Prime Minister. He had got the consent of the latter finally to the committing of the important documents, with the orders to the Western armies, to the care of a less conspicuous and more solid person—an uncle of his named Horne Hewitt, a rather colorless country squire who had been a good soldier, and was the military adviser of the committee. He was charged with expediting the government pledge, along with the concerted military plans, to the half-mutinous command in the west; and the still more urgent task of seeing that it did not fall into the hands of the enemy, who might appear at any moment from the east. Over and above this military official, the only other person present was a police official, a certain Doctor Prince, originally a police surgeon and now a distinguished detective, sent to be a bodyguard to the group. He was a square-faced man with big spectacles and a grimace that expressed the intention of keeping his mouth shut. Nobody else shared their captivity except the hotel proprietor, a crusty Kentish man with a crab-apple face, one or two of his servants, and another servant privately attached to Lord James Herries. He was a young Scotchman named Campbell, who looked much more distinguished than his bilious-looking master, having chestnut hair and a long saturnine face with large but fine features. He was probably the one really efficient person in the house.

After about four days of the informal council, March had come to feel a sort of grotesque sublimity about these dubious figures, defiant in the twilight of danger, as if they were hunchbacks and cripples left alone to defend a town. All were working hard; and he himself looked up from writing a page of memoranda in a private room to see Horne Fisher standing in the doorway, accoutered as if for travel. He fancied that Fisher looked a little pale; and after a moment that gentleman shut the door behind him and said, quietly:

"Well, the worst has happened. Or nearly the worst."

"The enemy has landed," cried March, and sprang erect out of his chair.

"Oh, I knew the enemy would land," said Fisher, with composure. "Yes, he's landed; but that's not the worst that could happen. The worst is that there's a leak of some sort, even from this fortress of ours. It's been a bit of a shock to me, I can tell you; though I suppose it's illogical. After all, I was full of admiration at finding three honest men in politics. I ought not to be full of astonishment if I find only two."

He ruminated a moment and then said, in such a fashion that March could hardly tell if he were changing the subject or no:

"It's hard at first to believe that a fellow like Herries, who had pickled himself in vice like vinegar, can have any scruple left. But about that I've noticed a curious thing. Patriotism is not the first virtue. Patriotism rots into Prussianism when you pretend it is the first virtue. But patriotism is sometimes the last virtue. A man will swindle or seduce who will not sell his country. But who knows?"

"But what is to be done?" cried March, indignantly.

"My uncle has the papers safe enough," replied Fisher, "and is sending them west to-night; but somebody is trying to get at them from outside, I fear with the assistance of somebody inside. All I can do at present is to try to head off the man outside; and I must get away now and do it. I shall be back in about twenty-four hours. While I'm away I want you to keep an eye on these people and find out what you can. Au revoir." He vanished down the stairs; and from the window March could see him mount a motor cycle and trail away toward the neighboring town.

On the following morning, March was sitting in the window seat of the old inn parlor, which was oak-paneled and ordinarily rather dark; but on that occasion it was full of the white light of a curiously clear morning—the moon had shone brilliantly for the last two or three nights. He was himself somewhat in shadow in the corner of the window seat; and Lord James Herries, coming in hastily from the garden behind, did not see him. Lord James clutched the back of a chair, as if to steady himself, and, sitting down abruptly at the table, littered with the last meal, poured himself out a tumbler of brandy and drank it. He sat with his back to March, but his yellow face appeared in a round mirror beyond and the tinge of it was like that of some horrible malady. As March moved he started violently and faced round.

"My God!" he cried, "have you seen what's outside?"

"Outside?" repeated the other, glancing over his shoulder at the garden.

"Oh, go and look for yourself," cried Herries in a sort of fury.

"Hewitt's murdered and his papers stolen, that's all."

He turned his back again and sat down with a thud; his square shoulders were shaking. Harold March darted out of the doorway into the back garden with its steep slope of statues.

The first thing he saw was Doctor Prince, the detective, peering through his spectacles at something on the ground; the second was the thing he was peering at. Even after the sensational news he had heard inside, the sight was something of a sensation.

The monstrous stone image of Britannia was lying prone and face downward on the garden path; and there stuck out at random from underneath it, like the legs of a smashed fly, an arm clad in a white shirt sleeve and a leg clad in a khaki trouser, and hair of the unmistakable sandy gray that belonged to Horne Fisher's unfortunate uncle. There were pools of blood and the limbs were quite stiff in death.

"Couldn't this have been an accident?" said March, finding words at last.

"Look for yourself, I say," repeated the harsh voice of Herries, who had followed him with restless movements out of the door. "The papers are gone, I tell you. The fellow tore the coat off the corpse and cut the papers out of the inner pocket. There's the coat over there on the bank, with the great slash in it."

"But wait a minute," said the detective, Prince, quietly. "In that case there seems to be something of a mystery. A murderer might somehow have managed to throw the statue down on him, as he seems to have done. But I bet he couldn't easily have lifted it up again. I've tried; and I'm sure it would want three men at least. Yet we must suppose, on that theory, that the murderer first knocked him down as he walked past, using the statue as a stone club, then lifted it up again, took him out and deprived him of his coat, then put him back again in the posture of death and neatly replaced the statue. I tell you it's physically impossible. And how else could he have unclothed a man covered with that stone monument? It's worse than the conjurer's trick, when a man shuffles a coat off with his wrists tied."

"Could he have thrown down the statue after he'd stripped the corpse?" asked March.

"And why?" asked Prince, sharply. "If he'd killed his man and got his papers, he'd be away like the wind. He wouldn't potter about in a garden excavating the pedestals of statues. Besides—Hullo, who's that up there?"

High on the ridge above them, drawn in dark thin lines against the sky, was a figure looking so long and lean as to be almost spidery. The dark silhouette of the head showed two small tufts like horns; and they could almost have sworn that the horns moved.

"Archer!" shouted Herries, with sudden passion, and called to him with curses to come down. The figure drew back at the first cry, with an agitated movement so abrupt as almost to be called an antic. The next moment the man seemed to reconsider and collect himself, and began to come down the zigzag garden path, but with obvious reluctance, his feet falling in slower and slower rhythm. Through March's mind were throbbing the phrases that this man himself had used, about going mad in the middle of the night and wrecking the stone figure. Just so, he could fancy, the maniac who had done such a thing might climb the crest of the hill, in that feverish dancing fashion, and look down on the wreck he had made. But the wreck he had made here was not only a wreck of stone.

When the man emerged at last on to the garden path, with the full light on his face and figure, he was walking slowly indeed, but easily, and with no appearance of fear.

"This is a terrible thing," he said. "I saw it from above; I was taking a stroll along the ridge."

"Do you mean that you saw the murder?" demanded March, "or the accident? I mean did you see the statue fall?"

"No," said Archer, "I mean I saw the statue fallen."

Prince seemed to be paying but little attention; his eye was riveted on an object lying on the path a yard or two from the corpse. It seemed to be a rusty iron bar bent crooked at one end.

"One thing I don't understand," he said, "is all this blood. The poor fellow's skull isn't smashed; most likely his neck is broken; but blood seems to have spouted as if all his arteries were severed. I was wondering if some other instrument . . . that iron thing, for instance; but I don't see that even that is sharp enough. I suppose nobody knows what it is."

"I know what it is," said Archer in his deep but somewhat shaky voice. "I've seen it in my nightmares. It was the iron clamp or prop on the pedestal, stuck on to keep the wretched image upright when it began to wobble, I suppose. Anyhow, it was always stuck in the stonework there; and I suppose it came out when the thing collapsed."

Doctor Prince nodded, but he continued to look down at the pools of blood and the bar of iron.

"I'm certain there's something more underneath all this," he said at last. "Perhaps something more underneath the statue. I have a huge sort of hunch that there is. We are four men now and between us we can lift that great tombstone there."

They all bent their strength to the business; there was a silence save for heavy breathing; and then, after an instant of the tottering and staggering of eight legs, the great carven column of rock was rolled away, and the body lying in its shirt and trousers was fully revealed. The spectacles of Doctor Prince seemed almost to enlarge with a restrained radiance like great eyes; for other things were revealed also. One was that the unfortunate Hewitt had a deep gash across the jugular, which the triumphant doctor instantly identified as having been made with a sharp steel edge like a razor. The other was that immediately under the bank lay littered three shining scraps of steel, each nearly a foot long, one pointed and another fitted into a gorgeously jeweled hilt or handle. It was evidently a sort of long Oriental knife, long enough to be called a sword, but with a curious wavy edge; and there was a touch or two of blood on the point.

"I should have expected more blood, hardly on the point," observed Doctor Prince, thoughtfully, "but this is certainly the instrument. The slash was certainly made with a weapon shaped like this, and probably the slashing of the pocket as well. I suppose the brute threw in the statue, by way of giving him a public funeral."

March did not answer; he was mesmerized by the strange stones that glittered on the strange sword hilt; and their possible significance was broadening upon him like a dreadful dawn. It was a curious Asiatic weapon. He knew what name was connected in his memory with curious Asiatic weapons. Lord James spoke his secret thought for him, and yet it startled him like an irrelevance.

"Where is the Prime Minister?" Herries had cried, suddenly, and somehow like the bark of a dog at some discovery.

Doctor Prince turned on him his goggles and his grim face; and it was grimmer than ever.

"I cannot find him anywhere," he said. "I looked for him at once, as soon as I found the papers were gone. That servant of yours, Campbell, made a most efficient search, but there are no traces."

There was a long silence, at the end of which Herries uttered another cry, but upon an entirely new note.

"Well, you needn't look for him any longer," he said, "for here he comes, along with your friend Fisher. They look as if they'd been for a little walking tour."

The two figures approaching up the path were indeed those of Fisher, splashed with the mire of travel and carrying a scratch like that of a bramble across one side of his bald forehead, and of the great and gray-haired statesman who looked like a baby and was interested in Eastern swords and swordmanship. But beyond this bodily recognition, March could make neither head nor tail of their presence or demeanor, which seemed to give a final touch of nonsense to the whole nightmare. The more closely he watched them, as they stood listening to the revelations of the detective, the more puzzled he was by their attitude—Fisher seemed grieved by the death of his uncle, but hardly shocked at it; the older man seemed almost openly thinking about something else, and neither had anything to suggest about a further pursuit of the fugitive spy and murderer, in spite of the prodigious importance of the documents he had stolen. When the detective had gone off to busy himself with that department of the business, to telephone and write his report, when Herries had gone back, probably to the brandy bottle, and the Prime Minister had blandly sauntered away toward a comfortable armchair in another part of the garden, Horne Fisher spoke directly to Harold March.

"My friend," he said, "I want you to come with me at once; there is no one else I can trust so much as that. The journey will take us most of the day, and the chief business cannot be done till nightfall. So we can talk things over thoroughly on the way. But I want you to be with me; for I rather think it is my hour."

March and Fisher both had motor bicycles; and the first half of their day's journey consisted in coasting eastward amid the unconversational noise of those uncomfortable engines. But when they came out beyond Canterbury into the flats of eastern Kent, Fisher stopped at a pleasant little public house beside a sleepy stream; and they sat down to eat and to drink and to speak almost for the first time. It was a brilliant afternoon, birds were singing in the wood behind, and the sun shone full on their ale bench and table; but the face of Fisher in the strong sunlight had a gravity never seen on it before.

"Before we go any farther," he said, "there is something you ought to know. You and I have seen some mysterious things and got to the bottom of them before now; and it's only right that you should get to the bottom of this one. But in dealing with the death of my uncle I must begin at the other end from where our old detective yarns began. I will give you the steps of deduction presently, if you want to listen to them; but I did not reach the truth of this by steps of deduction. I will first of all tell you the truth itself, because I knew the truth from the first. The other cases I approached from the outside, but in this case I was inside. I myself was the very core and center of everything."

Something in the speaker's pendent eyelids and grave gray eyes suddenly shook March to his foundations; and he cried, distractedly, "I don't understand!" as men do when they fear that they do understand. There was no sound for a space but the happy chatter of the birds, and then Horne Fisher said, calmly:

"It was I who killed my uncle. If you particularly want more, it was I who stole the state papers from him."

"Fisher!" cried his friend in a strangled voice.

"Let me tell you the whole thing before we part," continued the other, "and let me put it, for the sake of clearness, as we used to put our old problems. Now there are two things that are puzzling people about that problem, aren't there? The first is how the murderer managed to slip off the dead man's coat, when he was already pinned to the ground with that stone incubus. The other, which is much smaller and less puzzling, is the fact of the sword that cut his throat being slightly stained at the point, instead of a good deal more stained at the edge. Well, I can dispose of the first question easily. Horne Hewitt took off his own coat before he was killed. I might say he took off his coat to be killed."

"Do you call that an explanation?" exclaimed March. "The words seem more meaningless, than the facts."

"Well, let us go on to the other facts," continued Fisher, equably.

"The reason that particular sword is not stained at the edge with

Hewitt's blood is that it was not used to kill Hewitt."

"But the doctor," protested March, "declared distinctly that the wound was made by that particular sword."

"I beg your pardon," replied Fisher. "He did not declare that it was made by that particular sword. He declared it was made by a sword of that particular pattern."

"But it was quite a queer and exceptional pattern," argued March; "surely it is far too fantastic a coincidence to imagine—"

"It was a fantastic coincidence," reflected Horne Fisher. "It's extraordinary what coincidences do sometimes occur. By the oddest chance in the world, by one chance in a million, it so happened that another sword of exactly the same shape was in the same garden at the same time. It may be partly explained, by the fact that I brought them both into the garden myself . . . come, my dear fellow; surely you can see now what it means. Put those two things together; there were two duplicate swords and he took off his coat for himself. It may assist your speculations to recall the fact that I am not exactly an assassin."

"A duel!" exclaimed March, recovering himself. "Of course I ought to have thought of that. But who was the spy who stole the papers?"

"My uncle was the spy who stole the papers," replied Fisher, "or who tried to steal the papers when I stopped him—in the only way I could. The papers, that should have gone west to reassure our friends and give them the plans for repelling the invasion, would in a few hours have been in the hands of the invader. What could I do? To have denounced one of our friends at this moment would have been to play into the hands of your friend Attwood, and all the party of panic and slavery. Besides, it may be that a man over forty has a subconscious desire to die as he has lived, and that I wanted, in a sense, to carry my secrets to the grave. Perhaps a hobby hardens with age; and my hobby has been silence. Perhaps I feel that I have killed my mother's brother, but I have saved my mother's name. Anyhow, I chose a time when I knew you were all asleep, and he was walking alone in the garden. I saw all the stone statues standing in the moonlight; and I myself was like one of those stone statues walking. In a voice that was not my own, I told him of his treason and demanded the papers; and when he refused, I forced him to take one of the two swords. The swords were among some specimens sent down here for the Prime Minister's inspection; he is a collector, you know; they were the only equal weapons I could find. To cut an ugly tale short, we fought there on the path in front of the Britannia statue; he was a man of great strength, but I had somewhat the advantage in skill. His sword grazed my forehead almost at the moment when mine sank into the joint in his neck. He fell against the statue, like Caesar against Pompey's, hanging on to the iron rail; his sword was already broken. When I saw the blood from that deadly wound, everything else went from me; I dropped my sword and ran as if to lift him up. As I bent toward him something happened too quick for me to follow. I do not know whether the iron bar was rotted with rust and came away in his hand, or whether he rent it out of the rock with his apelike strength; but the thing was in his hand, and with his dying energies he swung it over my head, as I knelt there unarmed beside him. I looked up wildly to avoid the blow, and saw above us the great bulk of Britannia leaning outward like the figurehead of a ship. The next instant I saw it was leaning an inch or two more than usual, and all the skies with their outstanding stars seemed to be leaning with it. For the third second it was as if the skies fell; and in the fourth I was standing in the quiet garden, looking down on that flat ruin of stone and bone at which you were looking to-day. He had plucked out the last prop that held up the British goddess, and she had fallen and crushed the traitor in her fall. I turned and darted for the coat which I knew to contain the package, ripped it up with my sword, and raced away up the garden path to where my motor bike was waiting on the road above. I had every reason for haste; but I fled without looking back at the statue and the body; and I think the thing I fled from was the sight of that appalling allegory.

"Then I did the rest of what I had to do. All through the night and into the daybreak and the daylight I went humming through the villages and markets of South England like a traveling bullet, till I came to the headquarters in the West where the trouble was. I was just in time. I was able to placard the place, so to speak, with the news that the government had not betrayed them, and that they would find supports if they would push eastward against the enemy. There's no time to tell you all that happened; but I tell you it was the day of my life. A triumph like a torchlight procession, with torchlights that might have been firebrands. The mutinies simmered down; the men of Somerset and the western counties came pouring into the market places; the men who died with Arthur and stood firm with Alfred. The Irish regiments rallied to them, after a scene like a riot, and marched eastward out of the town singing Fenian songs. There was all that is not understood, about the dark laughter of that people, in the delight with which, even when marching with the English to the defense of England, they shouted at the top of their voices, 'High upon the gallows tree stood the noble-hearted three . . . With England's cruel cord about them cast.' However, the chorus was 'God save Ireland,' and we could all have sung that just then, in one sense or another.

"But there was another side to my mission. I carried the plans of the defense; and to a great extent, luckily, the plans of the invasion also. I won't worry you with strategics; but we knew where the enemy had pushed forward the great battery that covered all his movements; and though our friends from the West could hardly arrive in time to intercept the main movement, they might get within long artillery range of the battery and shell it, if they only knew exactly where it was. They could hardly tell that unless somebody round about here sent up some sort of signal. But, somehow, I rather fancy that somebody will."

With that he got up from the table, and they remounted their machines and went eastward into the advancing twilight of evening. The levels of the landscape were repeated in flat strips of floating cloud and the last colors of day clung to the circle of the horizon. Receding farther and farther behind them was the semicircle of the last hills; and it was quite suddenly that they saw afar off the dim line of the sea. It was not a strip of bright blue as they had seen it from the sunny veranda, but of a sinister and smoky violet, a tint that seemed ominous and dark. Here Horne Fisher dismounted once more.

"We must walk the rest of the way," he said, "and the last bit of all I must walk alone."

He bent down and began to unstrap something from his bicycle. It was something that had puzzled his companion all the way in spite of what held him to more interesting riddles; it appeared to be several lengths of pole strapped together and wrapped up in paper. Fisher took it under his arm and began to pick his way across the turf. The ground was growing more tumbled and irregular and he was walking toward a mass of thickets and small woods; night grew darker every moment. "We must not talk any more," said Fisher. "I shall whisper to you when you are to halt. Don't try to follow me then, for it will only spoil the show; one man can barely crawl safely to the spot, and two would certainly be caught."

"I would follow you anywhere," replied March, "but I would halt, too, if that is better."

"I know you would," said his friend in a low voice. "Perhaps you're the only man I ever quite trusted in this world."

A few paces farther on they came to the end of a great ridge or mound looking monstrous against the dim sky; and Fisher stopped with a gesture. He caught his companion's hand and wrung it with a violent tenderness, and then darted forward into the darkness. March could faintly see his figure crawling along under the shadow of the ridge, then he lost sight of it, and then he saw it again standing on another mound two hundred yards away. Beside him stood a singular erection made apparently of two rods. He bent over it and there was the flare of a light; all March's schoolboy memories woke in him, and he knew what it was. It was the stand of a rocket. The confused, incongruous memories still possessed him up to the very moment of a fierce but familiar sound; and an instant after the rocket left its perch and went up into endless space like a starry arrow aimed at the stars. March thought suddenly of the signs of the last days and knew he was looking at the apocalyptic meteor of something like a Day of judgment.

Far up in the infinite heavens the rocket drooped and sprang into scarlet stars. For a moment the whole landscape out to the sea and back to the crescent of the wooded hills was like a lake of ruby light, of a red strangely rich and glorious, as if the world were steeped in wine rather than blood, or the earth were an earthly paradise, over which paused forever the sanguine moment of morning.

"God save England!" cried Fisher, with a tongue like the peal of a trumpet. "And now it is for God to save."

As darkness sank again over land and sea, there came another sound; far away in the passes of the hills behind them the guns spoke like the baying of great hounds. Something that was not a rocket, that came not hissing but screaming, went over Harold March's head and expanded beyond the mound into light and deafening din, staggering the brain with unbearable brutalities of noise. Another came, and then another, and the world was full of uproar and volcanic vapor and chaotic light. The artillery of the West country and the Irish had located the great enemy battery, and were pounding it to pieces.

In the mad excitement of that moment March peered through the storm, looking again for the long lean figure that stood beside the stand of the rocket. Then another flash lit up the whole ridge. The figure was not there.

Before the fires of the rocket had faded from the sky, long before the first gun had sounded from the distant hills, a splutter of rifle fire had flashed and flickered all around from the hidden trenches of the enemy. Something lay in the shadow at the foot of the ridge, as stiff as the stick of the fallen rocket; and the man who knew too much knew what is worth knowing.

CPSIA information can be obtained
at www.ICGtesting.com
Printed in the USA
LVHW050619301122
734192LV00012B/387

9 781805 470229